RACE TO WALLABY BAY

Books by Robert Elmer

ADVENTURES DOWN UNDER

#1 / *Escape to Murray River*
#2 / *Captive at Kangaroo Springs*
#3 / *Rescue at Boomerang Bend*
#4 / *Dingo Creek Challenge*
#5 / *Race to Wallaby Bay*

THE YOUNG UNDERGROUND

#1 / *A Way Through the Sea*
#2 / *Beyond the River*
#3 / *Into the Flames*
#4 / *Far From the Storm*
#5 / *Chasing the Wind*
#6 / *A Light in the Castle*
#7 / *Follow the Star*
#8 / *Touch the Sky*

ROBERT ELMER

RACE TO WALLABY BAY

BETHANY HOUSE PUBLISHERS
MINNEAPOLIS, MINNESOTA 55438

Race to Wallaby Bay
Copyright © 1998
Robert Elmer

Cover illustration by Chris Ellison
Cover design by the Lookout Design Group

Scripture quotations are from the King James Version of the Bible.

Published by Bethany House Publishers
A Ministry of Bethany Fellowship International
11300 Hampshire Avenue South
Minneapolis, Minnesota 55438
www.bethanyhouse.com

Printed in the United States of America by
Bethany Press International, Minneapolis, Minnesota 55438

Library of Congress Cataloging-in-Publication Data

CIP data applied for

ISBN 0–7642–2103–5   CIP

To the mission-minded Brand family—

Joe and Julie,
plus Nathan, Gavin,
and Mallory

Meet Robert Elmer

ROBERT ELMER is the author of THE YOUNG UNDERGROUND series, as well as many magazine and newspaper articles. He lives with his wife, Ronda, and their three children, Kai, Danica, and Stefan (and their dog, Freckles), in a Washington State farming community just a bike ride away from the Canadian border.

CONTENTS

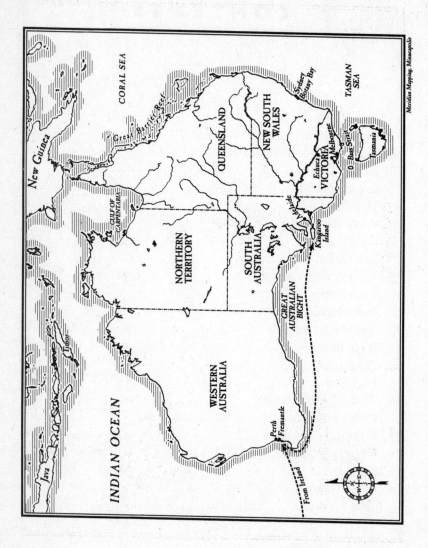

INDIAN OCEAN

New Guinea

CORAL SEA

Great Barrier Reef

GULF OF CARPENTARIA

Java

Timor

NORTHERN TERRITORY

QUEENSLAND

NEW SOUTH WALES

Sydney
Botany Bay

TASMAN SEA

WESTERN AUSTRALIA

SOUTH AUSTRALIA

Adelaide

Educa
VICTORIA
Melbourne
Bass Strait
Tasmania

Kangaroo Island

GREAT AUSTRALIAN BIGHT

Perth
Fremantle

From Ireland

Meridian Mapping, Minneapolis

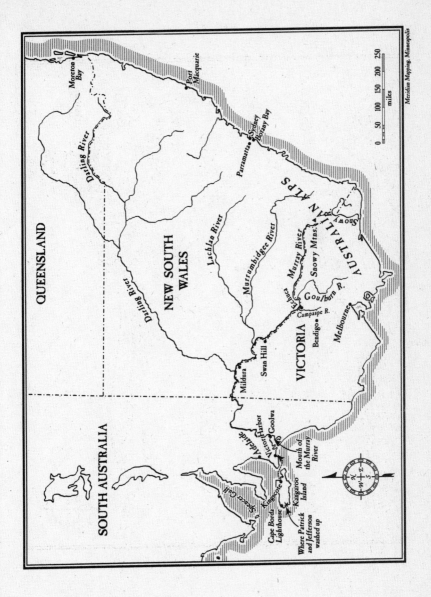

QUEENSLAND

SOUTH AUSTRALIA

NEW SOUTH WALES

Darling River

Darling River

Lachlan River

Murrumbidgee River

Murray River

VICTORIA

Moreton Bay

Port Macquarie

Parramatta • Sydney
Botany Bay

AUSTRALIAN ALPS

Snowy Mtns.

Goulburn R.

Echuca

Campaspe R.

Bendigo •

Melbourne

Swan Hill

Mildura

Adelaide

Victor Harbor
Goolwa

Mouth of
the Murray
River

Backstairs
Kangaroo
Island

Cape Borda
Lighthouse

Where Patrick
and Jefferson
washed up

AUSTRALIA

Snowy R.

Meridian Mapping, Minneapolis

miles

0   50   100 150 200 250

CHAPTER 1

CRY FOR HELP

Thirteen-year-old Patrick McWaid thought he was the first to hear the pounding noise. He shook his groggy head and sat up straight in his cot, listening in the darkness. And there it was again—a sharp rapping on the door of their cabin. Three times, *knock-knock-knock*, and then quiet. Across the cabin and behind the sheet that hung from the ceiling, his father still snored.

"Hello?" came a muffled voice from outside, then another knock. "Anyone home?"

Patrick flew out of his canvas cot before he knew what he was doing. His older sister, Becky, stumbled to her feet on the other side of the cabin. Without thinking, Patrick pulled the front door open wide to find a boy in his teens standing in front of him in the dim, early morning light. The boy held the reins to a hard-breathing brown horse in one hand and a letter in the other. Unlike Patrick, he had all his clothes on.

"Sorry," mumbled the boy, taking a step back. "They told me someone would be awake here."

Patrick looked down at himself for the first time, at his bare feet and the ripped, faded trousers he had slept in.

"We're awake," said Patrick, still a little confused.

"Patrick!" Becky hissed from inside. "Close that door. You can't stand there half dressed!"

"Oh." Finally it registered in Patrick's mind what he must look like to the visitor—shirtless and confused, as if he had just been washed down the river. He retreated back behind the door and peeked outside, feeling enormously silly, and shivered in the September spring chill coming through the open door. The boy waved a small envelope, but this time he was smiling.

"I have an urgent message for John McWaid," he said, pushing the envelope at Patrick. "Came in this morning. This the right place?"

"John McWaid's my pa." Patrick reached around as far as he could to take the letter. "I'll give it to him. Thank you."

That must have been fine with the message boy, who chuckled again and turned on his heel. He was back on his horse before Patrick could even close the door.

"What is it?" The groggy voice of their father came from the back of the cabin. "What's all the noise out there?"

Patrick didn't answer right off. With his eyes wide open and his cheeks still red, he skipped over to his bed, pulled on his clothes, and slipped his cold toes into a pair of shoes. He checked inside the shoes first, though, for spiders or other critters that might have taken shelter there overnight.

"A letter, Pa," Patrick finally answered. He studied the hasty scrawl on the outside of the envelope before he handed it over. It was addressed simply to "John McWaid, Erin's Landing, Echuca." Patrick knew right away it had to be from his grandpa, who was up the river repairing his paddle steamer, the *Lady Elisabeth*. Most anyone else from out of the area would have added "Victoria" or even "Australia" to the address.

"Ooh," squealed Becky, pulling a gray-flannel bathrobe around her shoulders. "I wonder who it's from, that it should be so urgent."

Patrick stood next to his father, where the dim light trickled in through the front windows—the ones shaped like those in the steering house of an old riverboat. Actually, that part of the cabin *was* the steering house taken off a retired riverboat, complete with wooden steering wheel. Patrick's grandpa had built the cabin for himself long before the rest of the McWaids showed up in Australia from Ireland several months before.

"Open it," urged their mother, getting up herself. She was slender and petite like her daughter, and she had also wrapped a heavy gray-flannel bathrobe around her tiny shoulders. The early spring nights still held a nip, but already the days were warming up quickly after a mild winter. Patrick had heard that's why the river was so high again—the snow was melting quickly up in the Snowy Mountains. But it was September—springtime—and it would still take some getting used to the upside-down seasons "down under" in Australia. Winter had come in June. And when Christmas came around in a few months, they would probably be sweating through the middle of the hot season. Who could figure it?

Patrick leaned over his father's shoulder to read while Mr. McWaid squinted at the single page he held in his hand. He seemed lost in the words of the letter he held. When Patrick looked over his shoulder again, he could see why.

"It's from Grandpa," Patrick told his sister. Even nine-year-old Michael was up by that time. Always the last to meet the day, he stood next to his cot and rubbed his puffy eyes.

"Look." Patrick pointed at the letter since his father didn't seem ready to read it out loud. "It's dated a week ago—August 25, 1868. It says, 'Dear son, I trust this note finds you in good—' "

" 'In good health.' " Mr. McWaid cleared his throat and took over the reading. He turned to his wife with a worried look. " 'I've hesitated writing to you, realizing you have your own family to care for. But I find myself needing another pair of strong hands to finish raising the *Lady Elisabeth*. Though I'm almost finished, the task has proven itself more difficult than I'd first imagined. And my crew . . .' "

There Patrick could see the writing was crossed out several times, as if his grandpa couldn't quite decide what to say.

" 'And my crew . . .' " continued their father. " 'I'll explain when you get here. Please make all haste to join me, and I'll be sure to pay you when I can, just as if you were a regular crewman.' "

"And then it's signed Patrick McWaid," finished Patrick. He smiled to see the name—his name, too. He was the "other" Patrick

McWaid, a fact that had helped them find their grandpa just a few months ago in this strange new land. It had taken several weeks and a long trip up the river, but they had found him. Their father, too, after a heart-stopping adventure that saw Mr. McWaid arrested in Ireland and sent to prison in far-off Australia, all for a crime he never committed.

"But, John, you can't go." Mrs. McWaid took the letter from her husband's hands and read it for herself. Her jaw tightened, and her pretty, sparkling green eyes flashed with anger as she read. "Now that we chased you halfway across the world, I'm not letting you out of my sight for a good, long while."

Patrick understood how his mother felt. But his father wasn't backing down.

"Ah, Sarah," objected Mr. McWaid. "You have to admit we were partly responsible for the sinking of the *Lady E*. D'you not think we should help raise her, as well?"

Patrick felt his neck grow hot and red as he looked away. He was sure his father hadn't meant to blame him, but he couldn't forget that he had been at the wheel of his grandpa's boat when they had been rammed by a log and sunk.

"Perhaps," admitted their mother, "but you promised me, John McWaid, that you wouldn't go running off alone again now that we're settled. After all the trouble we've been through? Really!"

"Sarah, don't you understand? He may be a cranky old man, but he's my father. And by the sound of it, he needs my help."

"You're not going, John, and that's the end of it." Mrs. McWaid sounded more than determined, but their father raised his eyebrows.

"Sarah, it's not the end of anything. Now, if you won't fix me a sack of food, I'll do it myself."

Mrs. McWaid's eyes filled with tears, and for a moment Patrick felt a flash of hot anger at his grandpa.

It's not fair, he thought. *He has a crew to help him. Now he has to drag Pa up there, too.*

"Why don't we all go?" piped up Michael. He had been standing quietly to the side, listening the whole while. "We can help, and Pa won't be alone."

Michael rolled up the sleeve of his wool shirt to show his lanky little arm, then flexed his muscle like a circus performer. Ma shook her head, but their father chuckled. Patrick felt his brother's arm and smiled.

"They'll miss school," insisted their mother.

"We'll bring some of our books with us, Ma," volunteered Becky.

Mr. McWaid put up his hands. "It's not a bad idea, you have to admit."

"I'll get our tools together," said Patrick, heading for the door.

His mother opened her mouth to object, but this time she was clearly outnumbered. "I'll pack us food for a few days," she sighed, and Michael clapped his hands.

"What about your work at the newspaper, Pa?" worried Becky.

Mr. McWaid scratched his chin. "For some reason Mr. Field at the *Herald* told me to take a few days off, so perhaps I'd best take him up on the offer. We'll leave this morning. In fact, I think the neighbor will lend us his wagon."

"Hmm." Mrs. McWaid wasn't satisfied, but her husband continued.

"And besides, my dear woman, from the sound of the letter, we'll be back in just a few days."

Patrick took another look at the letter and noticed something written in tiny handwriting along the bottom of the page—something his father had not read aloud.

Please hurry, Johnny, it said, like a forgotten postscript. *I'll explain everything when you arrive.*

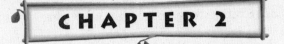

CHAPTER 2

RETURN TO BOOMERANG BEND

"Sorry about that." Mr. McWaid apologized once more as they nearly bottomed out on a bone-jarring bump in the road that took them upriver to the place called Boomerang Bend. Everyone held on as best they could, and Patrick gritted his teeth. Their neighbor Mr. Duggan's old horse paused for a moment before going on.

Up ahead in the late afternoon sun, if he followed the snaking line of blue-green eucalyptus trees that hugged the winding Murray River, Patrick could make out the place where the *Lady Elisabeth* lay helpless in the river mud.

Truth be told, he wasn't sure he wanted to see it just yet. Not if it was still caught in the current against a tangle of trees and river driftwood, more underwater than above. At least, that's how they had left it a few weeks ago. Patrick shuddered when he remembered the last time he had seen the proud little steamer, nearly belly-up and in danger of being turned to kindling by the sheer power of the flooded river.

What's it going to look like? Patrick bit his lip, trying not to think about the wreck or about how unfair it seemed that his father had to drop everything to help repair it. But the longer they rode, the more he thought.

Pa just comes running, fumed Patrick. *What if something happens and we lose him again?*

"Are you mad about something, Patrick?"

Patrick shook his head at his brother's question.

"But you're biting your lip," continued Michael, "the way you always do when you're mad. You're going to start bleeding."

"I told you I'm not angry."

"But you are."

"I am not."

Michael just looked up at Patrick, waiting for him to admit that he really *was* upset. Finally Patrick sighed and shook his head slowly.

"The whole thing's not fair, that's all."

"What?" Becky joined in. "Not fair that we're helping Grandpa?"

"No, I just don't think it's fair that he expects Pa to leave everything and come running."

"Patrick, how can you say such a thing? He needs help! Even *you* can see that."

"But what's going to happen to Pa? What about his job?"

"I don't know, Patrick." Becky shook her head. "Some things are just more important, that's all. I thought you would understand that."

"I *do* understand, Becky. It's just that . . ." Patrick couldn't finish the sentence. Was he the only one who felt this way about their grandpa—that he was asking too much? His father looked like he was glad to drop everything to come help.

Still, Becky made him feel guilty for saying anything. Somehow he knew he ought to feel different, but he couldn't help it.

Patrick glanced at his parents. His mother's head nodded like Becky's rag doll. Everyone was tired after many hours in the bumpy wagon. Their father still bravely gripped the reins.

"How are you doing, Pa?" asked Patrick, kneeling in the wagon bed behind his father.

But his father only nodded with the bump of the road.

"Pa?" Patrick stood up and gripped his father by the shoulders. Together they nearly toppled backward into the wagon.

"Whoa!" Patrick's father came to life, pulling back on the reins and straightening. Mr. Duggan's swaybacked horse reared in fright.

"Patrick!" Mrs. McWaid woke from her dozing. "Whatever are you doing?"

Patrick checked his father. "I thought Pa was going to fall off."

"I appreciate your concern, son." Their father turned back to the horse and settled himself. "But there's nothing to worry yourself about. We're almost to Boomerang Bend. It's just up that way."

Michael announced he would be the first to spot their grandpa. Holding tight to the back of the bench seat where their parents sat, he kept watch for a break between the trees, waiting to see the *Lady Elisabeth*.

"There!" shouted Michael, jumping up so suddenly that Christopher, his pet koala, fell to the bottom of the wagon.

But the koala was not noticed as they neared the thickening band of river trees. A man with a hammer in his hand stared at them from the distance, standing straight between two crooked trees, not moving.

"Surely that's not him," whispered Patrick as they all stared. The man's clothes were muddy and torn, and when they drew close enough, Patrick could make out enormous black shadows under the man's bloodshot eyes—as if he hadn't slept in weeks.

"I thought Grandpa told us he was fine." Michael picked up Christopher and held him tight as they rolled closer.

"You got my message, I gather," croaked Captain McWaid when they were near enough to hear him. He very much looked like his river nickname, the "Old Man." Still, a flicker of a smile played at his lips. It looked like the first time he had smiled in a long while.

Becky and Michael were the first to jump down from the wagon, and they ran straight into their grandpa's arms.

"There, now," crooned the Old Man. "I'm quite happy to see you two, as well." He took his son's hand and gave Mrs. McWaid a peck on the cheek while Patrick hung back.

"Say, Patrick," his father called to him. "Come say g'day to your grandpa."

Patrick sidled up and shook his grandpa's hand without looking him straight in the eye. The hand felt clammy and weak, not at all like the firm grip he remembered from only a few weeks ago.

"Glad to see you, boy." Patrick's grandpa held on to his hand, but Patrick thought he didn't mean the words. "Where's your American friend?"

The Old Man peeked into the wagon to make sure no one else was with them.

"Jefferson and Luke are gone for a week on a fishing trip down-river," explained Becky. "They were supposed to get back today, so we left a note for them to follow us. They should be here soon."

"*If* they can find this place," added Patrick.

"Jefferson and Luke should be a big help to us." Mr. McWaid nodded as he spoke. "But we thought it best to come as soon as we could."

"Luke?" Their grandpa hadn't met their aborigine friend from Kangaroo Island, the boy who had helped Patrick and Jefferson when they first arrived in Australia.

"You remember we told you about Luke." Patrick wished his friends were there, too. "He's the aborigine fellow who first brought us food when Jefferson and I washed up on Kangaroo Island."

"Ah yes." The Old Man nodded as if he remembered, but his eyes were as dim as a lantern that had run out of oil. Patrick was sure his grandpa did not remember.

When the Lady Elisabeth *sank here at Boomerang Bend*, thought Patrick, *it took the Old Man down with it*.

"We brought all the tools I could find in your shed." Mr. McWaid changed the subject. He pointed out a large wooden sea chest with rope handles. "Where should we put these things?"

The Old Man motioned to a couple of makeshift tents in the trees near the river. A cold fire pit divided the two areas, but there was only one bedroll to be seen, and very little else. A tin cup hung from a nail in one of the trees, and a frying pan next to the fire needed a good scrubbing. Patrick and his father carried the tools to the campsite.

"I don't understand," said Mrs. McWaid, looking around. She carried a black cooking pot to the fire pit and sniffed at the greasy frying pan. "Whatever have you been eating? And where's the rest of your help? I thought—"

"Gone," interrupted the Old Man, and everyone fell silent when they saw his serious expression. "My crew is gone. Every last one. And they're not coming back. Not even Prentice, who was with me for years."

Becky looked around the camp, her eyes wide. Quietly she tied their horse to a nearby tree.

"You said you just needed an extra pair of hands, Grandpa!" Michael crossed his arms and planted his foot. "You didn't say it was *this* bad."

"Perhaps I didn't. . . ." The Old Man gazed toward the river at the part of the *Lady E* that still showed above the muddy waters of the Murray. Half of the paddle steamer's main cabin—the part on the main deck—was underwater. On top of that they could see the wheelhouse, with the nameboard still proudly hanging by a single nail. Even the highest part of the boat had been underwater, too, at some point; Patrick could tell by the way the once-sparkling white paint was muddy and coffee-colored.

Reminds me of the washtub on Saturday night, he thought, *when everyone else is done getting their baths and it's my turn*.

Little eddies of water swirled around the part of the paddle steamer they could still see. Of course, the *Lady Elisabeth* was a pocket-size paddle steamer, even for the narrow Murray River. But it still seemed as if a lot of the boat lay hopelessly underwater.

"We had the hole patched and all was well until the pump broke," explained their grandpa. "Got the windows boarded up so we could pump. Then a wire rope snapped in Robinson's face. Injured him pretty bad. He left."

Becky gasped at the story. "What then?"

Patrick was almost afraid to hear.

"The boat shifted, then nearly rolled over, with another one of the fellows inside. We got him out, but things went from bad to worse."

"So they *all* left you, just because of a few accidents?" Mr. McWaid still couldn't believe it.

The Old Man nodded slowly. "Every one of them. Said the ship is haunted, jinxed, or some such foolishness."

"Foolishness is right," put in Mrs. McWaid. "Surely such talk's not fitting for Christians."

"Yes, well . . ." The Old Man cleared his throat and looked down. "Nearly got me to believing it. But I've been working on the pump here the past couple of days. Almost had it fixed when you came along."

The Old Man took a deep, ragged breath, as if he was about to cry.

"But why can't you just hire a new crew?" wondered Mr. McWaid.

"That's just it, Johnny." The Old Man was pleading with his eyes. "When the crew left, all the money the prince sent me disappeared."

"All of it?" echoed Mr. McWaid, his voice as soft as the water that flowed by them. "You think someone stole it? Why didn't you take it to the constable?"

"I . . . ah . . ." The Old Man stuttered, then looked down. His ears had turned red. "I'm not certain what I would have told him. My recollection of the time isn't what it should be."

"You're saying you don't remember what happened?" Mr. McWaid wrinkled his forehead.

"It's but a foolish old man's problem." The Old Man turned away and shook his head.

"I assume you've looked for this money?" Mr. McWaid wasn't going to let the matter drop so easily.

"I have. But the box where I kept it is gone. The crew's gone. At least *you're* here."

Patrick looked at his grandpa, more stooped and wrinkled than he had ever remembered seeing him, and at last understood a little better why they had come.

"All right, then." John McWaid crossed his arms and stared at the paddle steamer as if he could raise it with a glare. "What do we do first, Captain?"

Already Michael had run around to the jumble of tree branches, logs, and roots where the *Lady Elisabeth* had come to rest. No one saw him until he was halfway across, on his way to the hulk of the paddle steamer.

"Michael!" roared the Old Man, coming to life. "You get off there!"

Michael looked up from his balancing act with an impish grin on his face, waved his arms like a windmill, and plunged into the tangle of river junk with a shout.

CHAPTER 3

FAMILY CREW

Patrick was the first to reach the spot where Michael had disappeared into the tangle of branches. He balanced his way across on a couple of logs, then listened.

"Michael?" he shouted. "Where are you?"

At first he heard nothing, only the Old Man crashing in behind him.

"Did you find him, lad?" called out the Old Man, getting closer.

Patrick shook his head and put up his hand.

It's as if the trees swallowed him up, he told himself, holding the branches to keep from slipping. *Just so he doesn't slip under the water*. The trees he stood on felt as if they would break at any moment, and they were slimy with mud. No wonder Michael had slipped through the cracks in the moving raft of river driftwood.

"Michael!" he called out once more. At least he had a pretty good idea where his little brother had fallen. One more step and he would be there. . . .

Somewhere down in the jumbled branches, Patrick finally heard what he was listening for—a whimper that told him Michael was still all right. A rustle in the branches. By that time the Old Man was beside Patrick.

"Down there!" Patrick pointed at a flash of pale, frightened face, then they saw a hand reach up.

"Patrick!" whimpered Michael.

He was hanging almost upside down, having slipped between the tangled branches of two floating trees. His shirt had been skewered on the end of a broken-off branch, and the little boy waved helplessly. His legs were twisted painfully around behind him, and river water swirled only inches below his head. Patrick couldn't figure out how he had jammed himself into such a small space, or how he had slipped sideways into such a narrow cave of branches. But one thing was sure: They couldn't simply lift him straight out.

"There you are, lad." The Old Man braced himself above and tried to reach down. Out of the corner of his eyes, Patrick noticed his father was on his way across the logjam, too.

Michael could only wave his hands helplessly and cry while their grandpa tried his best to reach down. But it was too far and too slippery to follow him. The branch cracked halfway. Michael jerked and screamed.

"Hold still!" commanded their grandpa. That was the right advice, but Patrick wasn't sure it was enough. He could imagine what would happen if Michael fell headfirst into the water, trapped inside and under the maze of trees, roots, logs, and branches. The thought gave him an idea.

"Pa!" Patrick yelled back at his father, who was still trying to get across the logjam. "We'll need some rope!"

His father nodded and turned back around for the shore. The Old Man tried again to reach Michael. He succeeded only in breaking more branches above the frightened boy's head. Patrick wasn't sure he could rescue Michael; he *was* sure he couldn't do anything to save both Michael and his grandpa if they both fell in the water.

The trees shifted and Patrick slipped away to the side. His grandpa didn't notice, and his father was on the way with the rope. The branches cracked again.

"Grandpa!" shouted Michael, but his voice was hoarse.

Patrick slipped down into the water between two trees on the other side of the log where Michael had fallen. He didn't stop to think of what would happen if a branch caught him underwater. He just took a deep breath, ducked down, and groped his way through the dark water toward Michael.

This way, he told himself. *Has to be.*

A branch caught him in the face, blocking the way.

No, you don't. Patrick struggled to break it away but succeeded only in bending it to the side. Just when his lungs were starting to cry out for air, he managed to slip past. A dim gray light told him that the way above was clear, and he came to the surface, gasping.

"Patrick!" the Old Man cried from above. "What on earth are you doing down there?"

It was all Patrick could do to get his breath back as the branch Michael clung to finally cracked all the way and Patrick's brother came tumbling down into the water on top of him. The Old Man reached out desperately and almost fell in himself. Patrick grabbed at the slick log beside him and tried to hold on to Michael at the same time.

"I'm right here, Michael." Patrick tried to sound like his father, tried to make his voice sound deep and powerful. "Pa will be here in a minute with a rope to help us up."

Michael held on to Patrick's neck, riding up as high as he could.

"I'm sorry, Patrick." His teeth chattered, and Patrick noticed the bone-chilling cold of the river water for the first time.

"Shh." Patrick looked up for the rope loop that hit him in the face. By that time both his father and grandpa were perched above them, looking down.

"Here he comes." Patrick helped Michael pull the looped rope over his shoulders and tried to push from below as best he could.

Mr. McWaid looked seriously from Patrick to Michael. Their clothes steamed on a clothesline next to the roaring fire, and both boys shivered under blankets as their mother and Becky fixed a hot dinner stew of carrots and potatoes.

"All right, that little incident tells us how dangerous it is to climb out on the logjam, does it not?"

Michael didn't answer, but Patrick guessed he wasn't going out there again soon. He looked at the outline of the half-sunk *Lady Elisabeth* and wondered how they were going to get her floating again. But their father had already taken charge of the situation.

"We're starting over," he decided, looking around at his crew. "We have plenty of time."

Their grandpa shook his head again.

"What now?" asked Mr. McWaid.

The Old Man cleared his throat. "I'm afraid I didn't tell you the whole story."

Patrick groaned quietly. *What could be worse than this?*

"I . . . ah . . . sold a half share in the vessel a time back. Money for repairs . . ."

"Oh." Their father sighed with relief. "Is that all?"

The Old Man shook his head but would not look at them. He studied the darkening shape of the *Lady Elisabeth*, as Patrick had done. "No, it's not all. I agreed to deliver the boat to the new investor in Goolwa by the end of the month, or lose the other half."

"Or *what*?" thundered Mr. McWaid. "You're telling me that you lose the entire boat if we don't raise it up now and scoot all the way down the river by the end of the month? That's thirty days!"

"That's what I'm telling you, Johnny." The Old Man nodded like a schoolboy who hadn't turned in his lesson. "Now do you see why I called you for help? I didn't know what else to do, other than just walk away from her." He closed his eyes and clenched his teeth. "I already did that once."

Patrick wasn't sure what his grandpa was talking about.

"But it can't be done!" insisted Mr. McWaid, pacing back and forth in their camp. "We could be pumping here day and night and still not . . . Well, it's going to take weeks just to refloat the beast. And how are we going to patch the hole in the side?"

"But we have to *try*, Pa," said Michael.

Patrick looked up at the heavy canvas tarp above their heads, then back at the *Lady Elisabeth*. A picture started to form in his head. *Maybe . . .*

"I think I have an idea," he announced, running his hand along the edge of the canvas. "Here's what we do. . . ."

The hardest part would be pulling the big square of canvas in place, Patrick knew, especially since the *Lady E* lay at such a crazy angle, stuck in the Murray River mud. But with a rope at each corner, they tugged and wrestled the giant patch over the hole.

"Do you really think this will work?" asked Becky, struggling with her corner.

The Old Man just grunted and tugged. Mr. McWaid was on the opposite side of the boat, chest deep in river water and struggling to keep his balance.

"Be careful, John!" shouted their mother from the shore. "The deck is slippery."

"Thanks for the hint." He grinned back at his wife.

"And, Patrick," she ignored the teasing, "you hold on there, too."

Patrick looked at the deck sloping away in front of his feet. If he let go, he would surely go sliding away and into the river.

"We've got it, Ma," he called back.

"All right," grunted their grandpa. "It's in place. Now we just have to keep it there."

"How about some nails around the edge?" asked Patrick.

The Old Man nodded. "I thought of the same thing. Problem is, I'll need to get into the water to get close enough."

The Old Man started to pull off his shirt, but Patrick was too quick. Before anyone else could stop him, Patrick had grabbed a hammer and a handful of nails from a bucket in the wheelhouse and slipped over the side.

"Patrick," objected his father, "you've already proven you're a brave enough lad. You don't need to prove it all over again."

"I'm already wet." Patrick waved back at his father. The Old Man frowned but threw a rope for Patrick to hold while he was in the water.

"Just a few nails along the edges," grunted the Old Man. "Just enough to keep it in place."

Patrick nodded and swung his hammer with one hand while

holding on as best he could with the other. The canvas patch wasn't pretty, but it looked as if it would do the job of holding out the water—at least for a time. And if they could pump out all the water that now filled the insides of the *Lady Elisabeth*, they had a chance of floating away.

"It's still a shame about the money," said Patrick, taking another swing. Three or four more nails and it would be secure. "If only we had—"

"If only!" thundered the Old Man, but he looked more angry at himself than at Patrick. "It's gone, and there's no good to be had from reliving the past."

"I didn't mean anything by it," Patrick whispered. His ears burned, and he wished he could take it back. He finished his nailing without another word and climbed back up to the deck.

"There you go." His father patted him on the back. "Now we just have to pump the water out, and we'll be on our way."

"That'll be no small matter, Johnny," muttered the Old Man. Looking down at all the water that filled the boat, Patrick knew his grandpa was right. But something else was not. Logs were groaning and rubbing against each other, all around the boat.

That was too easy, Patrick told himself, checking his patch once more. *If we could do all that in an afternoon, why couldn't the crew before us?*

Patrick got his answer perhaps sooner than he wanted as he looked to the shore to see his mother waving both her arms wildly.

"Boys!" she yelled, louder than Patrick had ever heard her yell before. "The rope is breaking loose!"

CHAPTER 4

IMPOSSIBLE JOB

Mrs. McWaid's warning was too late, even though the big rope that held the *Lady Elisabeth* in place hadn't snapped as Patrick first thought.

"It's the logjam," cried the Old Man. "It's breaking up again!"

"Again?" wondered Mr. McWaid.

He had no sooner finished the words when the boat shuddered and spun in the foaming river. Patrick was thrown to his knees as the *Lady Elisabeth* seemed to come to life, bumping and then nearly rolling across the riverbed, still filled with water. All around them the logs the paddle steamer had once been wedged into jostled and bumped the boat as if it were a part of a huge, seething stew.

Michael ran down the bank alongside them, waving his arms and screaming.

A lot of good that does, thought Patrick, gripping the side of the wheelhouse.

"Don't worry, now." The Old Man pointed at a heavy rope that had stretched tight between them and a tree on the shore. "The line there will hold us."

Patrick wasn't so sure as he watched the line tighten and hum like a violin string. The tree they were tied to shook and swayed, even though it seemed so thick that Patrick probably couldn't

31

reach his arms around it. But for now the Old Man was right—they were still anchored to the shore, and coming closer all the time.

"Closer!" yelled Michael, waving them on. Patrick held on as the *Lady E* dragged slowly to the side and tilted almost to within jumping distance of the soggy shore. The Old Man smiled weakly for the first time since they arrived.

"This is a sight better," he announced. "All that work we did to right the boat these past weeks, pullin' and tuggin' until we were blue in the face, we were. Now you people come and the river pushes us around, just like that."

"Maybe your 'jinx' is over," said Patrick's father with a grin.

"I doubt it." The Old Man surveyed his boat and pushed a plank across to the shore. "But we *are* a bit higher in the water. Patrick, step lively. I've two big pumps that we'll need to man."

Patrick hesitated; he thought he saw a horse in the distance through the trees.

"Did you hear me?" barked the captain. "Don't be standing there, staring like a statue, Patrick. I left her once, but I'm not going to leave her again!"

As Patrick tried to understand what he meant, the horse drew closer and they all saw who was approaching.

"Hi-oh!" shouted a powerful-looking young man from the front of a jet-black horse. Stocky and square-faced, his muscled arms held the reins lightly and his brown eyes twinkled when he smiled. Another boy hung on behind him, his skin almost as dark as the horse's hide. He was smaller and more slender than his light-skinned friend, but he looked just as much at home on the back of the horse. Both wore faded denim sailor's pants, a little frayed along the cuffs, and a pullover blue jersey.

"It's Jefferson and Luke!" Michael whirled around from where he stood watching and ran up to the approaching horse. The powerfully built fellow at the reins swung off easily and gave him a friendly pat on the shoulders.

"The great fishermen return!" Mrs. McWaid greeted the boys with a smile. "You found us all right?"

Jefferson spread his muscled arms wide and turned around. He smiled when he noticed Becky standing back by the Old Man's camp. "We found it, sure. Luke held the map and showed me where to go. He could find his way around anywhere. Me, I'm still feeling a long way from Arkansas."

Luke, always the shy one, hadn't said anything yet, but he smiled almost as widely as Jefferson when he held up a string of large, fat fish with light, leopard-like spots and long, narrow snouts. Murray River codfish.

"We caught a few," he announced.

"Fifteen," added Jefferson. He caught the fish when Luke tossed them down from the horse. "And guess who caught every fish but the two smallest ones?"

Luke shook his head and joined them on the ground. Grinning shyly, he led their horse to a tree.

"He's incredible," continued Jefferson. "One after the other, and all I could do was sit there, watching them get away."

"You just have to be patient." Luke smiled and handed the fish to Mrs. McWaid. "For dinner? They're pretty tasty."

Mrs. McWaid smiled and turned to her father-in-law. "I'm sorry for not introducing you to Luke. He's—"

"The young friend of old Boomer Gates!" interrupted the Old Man, grabbing Luke's hand. "It's good to finally meet you, Luke."

Luke nodded and looked down, letting the Old Man look at his hand.

"Fish scales," whispered Luke. "I'm sorry."

"Eeuw." Becky stepped over and held her nose. "I thought I smelled something."

"We kept them in cool water as long as we could." Jefferson reached out his hand to Patrick. "So how is the ship-raising, Patrick?"

Patrick shrugged and looked to his father.

"We're ready to pump," explained Mr. McWaid.

"And just thirty days—counting today—to reach Goolwa," put in the Old Man, wiping the fish smell off on his pants. He patted the side of the *Lady Elisabeth* fondly. "Now that we're all here and

33

introduced, let's not waste any more time chatting."

Patrick wasn't sure which was worse—fighting the mosquitoes or pumping the water out of the *Lady Elisabeth*.

"Scat!" he hissed, swatting at a persistent buzz that wanted to explore his ear. At the other pump Jefferson was doing the same—only his big arms were working the long up-and-down handle much faster. *He can pump more with one arm than I can with two.* But Patrick kept his handle moving. They were pumping the water out of the boat, he knew, but slowly. Very slowly.

"Race you," said Jefferson, grinning across at him. Patrick tried to grin back, but his arms took all his strength.

At the same time Becky and her father were using buckets to help speed the work, and the Old Man tinkered with the steam engine, which was barely above the water. Luke helped him shovel out the mud from the boiler as he waited for his turn to pump. Jefferson motioned to the Old Man with his chin and grinned.

"I had a captain like him once," he whispered to Patrick. "He's just wanting to get his ship out of the water, where it belongs."

Patrick nodded and kept pumping. Back on shore, Patrick could see his mother had just dished up several steaming tin plates piled high with fish.

"Dinner break!" she announced, but Patrick and Jefferson only pumped and swatted harder. Patrick was afraid of stopping first. He tried dancing and wiggling to keep out of the insects' way, but he couldn't avoid the swarms that covered his head.

"You think these mozzies are bad," said the Old Man, using the Australian slang for mosquitoes, "but you weren't here, oh, what was it? Five years ago, as I recall."

He casually flattened another of the insects perched on his arm, flicked it off, and continued. Jefferson and Patrick listened to the story as they pumped.

"'Twas a wet spring, almost as wet as this one, and we were

halfway to Swan Hill, dragging a good-sized barge. We were two days behind schedule, as a matter of fact."

Mrs. McWaid came to the riverbank, her hands on her hips. Patrick knew she was waiting for them to come up to their meal, to eat together, but he didn't dare interrupt the Old Man.

"At one point the mozzies were so big and so thick that a number of 'em drilled their way through the side of the boat. Me being inside steering, I picked up a hammer and pounded their noses down flat, see? Just like a big row of nails, it was."

"How many?" gasped Michael, following his grandpa's every move.

"A score," replied the Old Man. "No, 'twas closer to fifty or a hundred. But they were big as crows, they were, and a hundred times as fierce."

"What happened then?" Michael stood with a bucket in his hands. Patrick looked for a flicker of a grin on his grandpa's drawn face, but there was none.

"Well, those mozzies were so fired-up angry," said the Old Man, "they took the poor *Lady Elisabeth* in tow. Lifted us clear out of the water a good two, three inches. We made Swan Hill two days ahead of schedule, flying just above the water all the way."

Jefferson put his hand over his mouth and chuckled. Luke grinned and shook his head as he jumped to shore. Michael's mouth dropped.

"Grandpa!" he said. "I thought you were telling me a true story."

"You don't believe me?" The corners of the Old Man's mouth twitched, but still he didn't smile. "Just look at the row of holes in the boat there in the wheelhouse."

Michael started to scramble across the board bridge they had set up to the swamped *Lady Elisabeth* to see for himself, but his mother caught him by the back of the shirt.

"You can look for insects after your dinner, young man," she told him. "Right now your fish is getting cold. And I think perhaps those mosquitoes your grandpa is telling you about may have already carried it off."

"There was more to the story, Sarah," explained the Old Man, holding up his hand. But then he lowered it again with a puzzled expression on his face. "Only I can't seem to recall what it is just now. . . ."

He stood on the top of the cabin, put his hands to the sides of his head, and swayed. His knees seemed to fold beneath him, but he caught himself.

"Grand—" Patrick reached out, but his grandpa waved him off gruffly.

"No, no. Just a wee headache, that's all."

Jefferson was back to concentrating on his pumping, but Becky turned and frowned.

"I'll bring you some dinner out here, Grandpa," she said.

When the food arrived, Patrick ate as he pumped, afraid to slow down. By that time he had almost given up on the mosquitoes. Luke had taken over on the other pump, and Becky returned to the buckets.

"We're making progress, don't you think?" asked their aborigine friend. He seemed to have no trouble keeping up with Patrick.

Patrick tried to see if the waterline had gone down at all, but he could barely see it through one of the windows. Although most of the cabin was above water, everything was covered with a thick layer of Murray River silt and slime.

"Looks about the same to me. This is going to take weeks."

"Cheer up." Becky aimed a bucket of water his direction, and the Old Man returned to his steam engine.

This time, though, the captain of the *Lady Elisabeth* only muttered and pounded on the machinery. He poked the tip of a large oil can into the joints and crevices, trying to chase away the rust and the mud. As evening dropped over the river and the mosquitoes grew even more fierce, he slammed his fist on the metal boiler, as if trying to threaten it back to life. Patrick looked around for a hammer in case his grandpa's story about the mosquitoes had been true.

That one on my neck is as big as he said they were, he told himself. *Maybe it wouldn't be so bad if we could just lift up the boat a few inches.*

He felt a tap on his shoulder—his father coming to relieve him of pump duty—then gratefully staggered back to shore. His throbbing arms felt almost disconnected from the rest of his body.

"Good bit of exercise, eh?" Jefferson met him as he shuffled into camp. A cloud of insects swarmed around the oil lantern, so Patrick hung back in the shadows and rubbed his sore arms.

"We can't keep this up," mumbled Patrick. "I don't see how we're going to make it."

"Sure, why not? We have thirty days, remember?"

"It's going to take us more than that just to pump out all this water." Patrick thought his older friend sounded a little too cheerful. "Even if Luke keeps it up twenty-four hours a day."

"No, no. A week at the most to finish pumping."

"Fine, but you don't understand," Patrick tried to tell him. "My grandpa's acting like a bully dictator. He abandoned Pa thirty years ago, and now he just marches right back in and thinks he can be the head of the family again. Well, it doesn't work that way!"

Jefferson's eyes grew wide in surprise at the sudden outburst, and even Patrick clapped his hand over his mouth at the things he'd said. Where had that all come from?

"I didn't mean it," Patrick whispered, feeling sheepish and embarrassed.

"Hmm. So you're not about to forget what your grandpa did before you were even born, is that it?"

Patrick wished Jefferson was wrong, but he wasn't.

"Well, can't say that I blame you overly much," continued the other boy. "Maybe I would have said the same thing if I were you."

They were interrupted by the sound of arguing from down on the *Lady Elisabeth*, at first soft, then getting louder. The boys looked at each other, and Patrick put a finger to his lips.

"Why didn't you let us help you before this instead of trying to do it all yourself?" asked Mr. McWaid, his voice drifting up from the water. "Before you went off and sold half the boat? We're your family, or have you forgotten already?"

The Old Man grumbled in reply; Patrick tried to hear but couldn't quite make out what he said. But he thought it sounded something like, "Ah, I'm too old to care anymore."

"Well, *we* care!" Mr. McWaid's voice was definitely louder this time. "You look terrible, for one thing."

"Don't you worry what I look like. I've never won any beauty contests, and you know it."

"We're not talking about beauty. It's your health I'm concerned about. What about those headaches?"

"That's my business and mine alone." The Old Man's voice came through a little louder, sounding a bit more stubborn.

"Tell me this, then, Father. Where did you find that character who made off with all the prince's money?"

"I told you before. We still don't know it was him. Or if it was actually stolen. All I know is—"

"It's simple enough to add two and two. You said yourself . . ."

As the arguing continued, Patrick peeked down at the *Lady E* and saw that the pumping had stopped. Luke must have abandoned ship when the arguing started, and Patrick didn't blame him. Instead, he could see a flickering gold and orange flame—not from a lantern, but from a small fire his grandpa had started in the firebox of the steam engine. The flames cast strange shadows of the two men down on the boat, long heads and stretched-out bodies.

"Well, it certainly wasn't Prentice who took the money. You know that. What was the new fellow's name? Judas Warbuckle?"

"War*burton*," the Old Man corrected him. "*Jonas* Warburton. He seemed to know the river."

"Yes, well, it seems he knows how to make off with someone's money, as well. I'll bet he's the thief."

"Now, wait—"

"Why can't you face the truth? I still don't know why you didn't go to the constable for help right when it happened."

A hissing sound filled the air, and the metal door of the firebox under the steam engine slammed shut. Patrick didn't hear his grandpa's reply, but it didn't sound pleasant. Neither did the loud pop that followed, louder than a gunshot and almost like a cannon exploding.

CHAPTER 5

THE PLAN

"What was that?" Becky shouted from the other side of the camp. Patrick imagined the steam boiler blowing up, or worse. He flew down to the *Lady Elisabeth* with the others on his heels.

"John!" cried Mrs. McWaid, picking up her skirts and running as fast as she could toward the river.

"Pa!" shouted Patrick. He stumbled onto a part of the slick deck that was barely above water, then lost his balance and slid feet first up to the doorway. At the last minute he managed to hook his arms over the main salon doorway ledge and crawl through.

In the lamplight his father and grandpa stared wide-eyed at them. Behind them, the steam engine puffed and wheezed, and a big green metal wheel on the side slowly turned.

"Patrick?" Mr. McWaid reached out his hand to help his son off the floor.

"You're all right!" exclaimed Patrick. Jefferson was the next to scramble on board, then Mrs. McWaid.

"Of course we're all right!" fumed the Old Man. "Have ye never heard an old steam engine starting up before?"

The engine was sputtering and popping. The paddle steamer shuddered as it struggled to come back to life.

"We just thought . . ." began Becky.

"Ahh . . ." The Old Man dismissed them with a wave of his hand. "You're frettin' about nothing."

Mr. McWaid shrugged at them as if to say, "What can I do?"

"We just weren't expecting to hear a small explosion." Mrs. McWaid backed down the boarding plank and returned to camp. Becky and Jefferson followed. But Patrick didn't move; he just stared at the spinning wheel on the side of the steam engine, then back at the pump handle in his father's hands, then back at the wheel once more. Even though the paddle wheels on either side of the boat had started to churn up the river, the paddle steamer wasn't going anywhere. It was still tied securely to the big tree on the shore. And much of the inside of the boat was still filled with dark river water.

But here is the steam engine, thought Patrick, looking at the pump his father held. *And there is the handle. If we could just connect the two . . .*

"Pa?" Patrick stepped closer. "I have an idea. If we could attach the pump handle like so . . ."

His father squinted and listened carefully to Patrick.

"Look, the wheel goes around and around like this." Patrick pointed out to his father while the Old Man looked on. "All we need to do is attach the pump handle to the wheel, and every time it comes around, it will push the pump. See?"

"Not bad." His father smiled as he watched Patrick. "I believe I've seen something like that before, back home in Dublin. Why didn't I think of it?"

Good idea or not, it still took a few hours of trying new ways to attach the pump handles to the spinning wheel on the side of the steam engine.

"All we have to do is find out a way to keep the rope from constantly breaking," said Mr. McWaid.

The Old Man just shook his head. "I still don't think it's a good idea," he told them with a frown. "All this time we could have been pumping. It's not going to work."

"It *will* work," insisted Mr. McWaid as he tied the end of the pump handle to the wheel with a short length of stronger rope. " 'Twas a good idea Patrick had."

Patrick avoided his grandpa's look while he and Luke helped his father. Jefferson kept on with the spare pump, splashing out a steady but slow stream of water. Finally they were ready to try again.

"Start it up," Mr. McWaid said. The Old Man frowned but turned the handle on the valve that sent steam shooting through the right pipe. Slowly, the wheel began turning as the steam hissed around them. But this time the pump handle was well connected, and a gush of water coiled through the fire hose like a living thing, through the door and over the side. Luke and Jefferson cheered and clapped.

"How about that!" Mr. McWaid grinned at his son, who shook his hand with a flourish. "Turn up the steam, Captain McWaid, and we'll have this vessel of yours pumped out overnight!"

The Old Man kept an eye on the spinning wheel but did as his son asked.

"Even if it does hold out," he said, wiping his hands on an oily rag, " 'twill take forty-eight hours at the least. I'll let you know when the rope breaks."

"Now, aren't you the cheery one?" asked Mr. McWaid. "Here your grandson figures out a way to help, and you act as if he's done you harm."

Patrick looked for the door, eager to put some distance between him and his grumpy grandpa.

After an hour of trying, Patrick decided he was too tired to sleep. So he lay still and listened to the humming of the mosquitoes, the popping cough of the steam engine, the splash of water being pumped out from two big pumps, and the gentle swish of the churning paddle wheels. The Old Man would get no sleep, either, tending the boiler's fire as if it were a crying infant.

"You should let me tend the fire for a couple of hours," said Mr.

McWaid, and once again, his voice carried up from the paddle steamer to the camp.

"Please don't argue anymore," whispered Patrick. He rolled over and held the thin blanket tight to his ears so he wouldn't hear. He tried praying but couldn't think of what to say to God.

Maybe you already know what I need, Patrick prayed, too tired to know for sure.

"There they go again," sighed Luke. He had been lying a few feet away in the darkness.

"Are you awake, too?" asked Patrick. He swatted at the mosquito in his ear and added a silent "amen" to his prayer.

"I've been thinking," Luke said. "What if we can catch up with this Warburton? He's the one your father thinks stole the money, right?"

"We don't even know what he looks like." Patrick wiggled his shoulders to avoid a pea-sized rock that had been playing hide-and-seek with his shoulder blades. "And besides, he could be anywhere. Upriver, downriver . . . maybe out in the bush. He could be all the way to Melbourne by now."

"Maybe so. But I'm guessing if that bloke suddenly has a lot of money in his pockets, he's going to go to the first place he can spend it."

"Echuca!" This time Patrick sat up. Maybe Luke was right. He looked at the bedroll where Jefferson was curled up, reached over, and shook his shoulder.

"Jeff!" he whispered in the other boy's ear. "Wake up."

"I wouldn't do that . . ." began Luke, too late. Before Patrick knew what hit him, Jefferson had swung his big right hand around, catching Patrick in the cheek.

"Ohh!" groaned Patrick, falling over on the ground.

"What's the matter with you?" Jefferson rubbed his eyes. "There was a huge mosquito right there in my face . . . in my ear. I think I got him."

"That wasn't a mosquito, Jeff," Luke told him. "That was Patrick."

"Really?" Jefferson didn't sound fully awake. "Sorry about that. What time is it?"

"Midnight, maybe." Luke helped Patrick sit back up, and Patrick gingerly touched a finger to his cheek.

"Listen, Jefferson," said Patrick. "We have a plan."

"We?" mumbled Becky from across the fire. "Patrick McWaid, it sounds like you're up to no good."

"Tell us," suggested Jefferson.

Patrick swatted mosquitoes as he listened to Luke explain his plan to recover the Old Man's money. For a moment it sounded so possible that Patrick caught himself looking into the shadows for signs of Warburton. He had to remind himself that the man certainly wouldn't come back to the camp—not after he had run off with so much money.

"Maybe we could spread the rumor around some of the river towns that there's more money on the *Lady Elisabeth*," suggested Luke. "We do that, and the villain shows up and . . ."

"And what?" wondered Patrick.

"And that's when we call the law," Luke decided. "Don't you think?"

"But that wouldn't be telling the truth to say something like that," said Becky. Patrick had considered the same thing.

Luke frowned and paused. "I hadn't thought of it quite that way."

"You're not serious, are you?" Jefferson stood up. "You don't worry about that sort of thing when you're fighting criminals."

"I do," said Becky quietly.

"Well, then," Jefferson challenged them. "Think of something better."

"Hmm." Luke rubbed his chin as if trying to come up with another plan.

Something better, Patrick repeated as he padded down to the riverbank. *Like not trying to find Warburton at all.*

Patrick heard a murmuring, then he saw a fire flickering on the *Lady Elisabeth* as his grandpa opened the firebox to throw in another piece of wood.

But I thought Pa came back to camp, he wondered to himself. *So who is the Old Man talking to?*

There had to be someone else. Patrick was sure he could hear more than one voice. Trying not to make a sound, he tiptoed closer, squishing the mud through his toes.

Inside the *Lady Elisabeth* the Old Man was stripped to the waist, and his chest glistened with sweat. He took pieces of split willow from the stack of wood they had piled there earlier in the day, out of reach of the water that still lapped in the boat. With a stick he pried open the door to the firebox and stuffed the wood into the heart of the flames.

Patrick looked more closely, but he could see no one else. Only the Old Man, and he looked very, very old, stooped and shaking. He was repeating something, too, over and over—as if he was speaking to the fire or to the boat. When Patrick took another step nearer, he could finally make out what his grandpa was saying.

"I'll never leave you again, Elisabeth," said the Old Man. "Never."

By that time Becky had followed and was right behind Patrick. But a crash from inside made him jump, and Patrick looked around to see his grandpa crumpled on the floor.

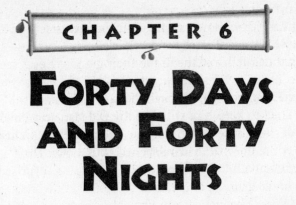

CHAPTER 6

FORTY DAYS AND FORTY NIGHTS

"Grandpa!" cried Becky. She and Patrick pushed into the tiny engine room. Their grandpa looked up at them with a mask of confusion.

"Elisabeth?" he cried, wild-eyed. Becky pulled back while Patrick slipped in and cradled his grandpa's head.

"Elisabeth?" the Old Man repeated, holding out his hand. "I told you I wouldn't leave you."

"It's Becky, Grandpa." Becky looked scared. "You fell. Are you all right?"

Their grandpa worked his jaw up and down as if he were trying to say something, then stared hard at Patrick.

"I *told* you to care for your mother, didn't I?" His voice quivered, almost out of control. "I *told* you before they took me away, but you let her die! I hold you responsible, young man!"

Patrick shook his head. "Ma's not dead. What are you talking about, Grandpa?"

That was when Patrick realized what the Old Man was saying. The Old Man was looking at Becky, but he saw his wife. The grandmother they had never known, the one who had died shortly after their grandpa had been taken away to Australia on a prison ship. And when he looked at Patrick, he was seeing their father—the boy

47

who had been left behind in Ireland, so many years ago, before they were born.

"Grandpa!" Becky was crying, and her tears fell on the Old Man's cheek. "It's just Becky and Patrick."

Another tear fell, and the fire in their grandpa's eyes seemed to fade.

"Becky?" he croaked. "Becky, what are you doing?"

They tried to keep him still, but the Old Man scrambled to his feet and dusted himself off. Somehow, thought Patrick, they would have to tell him what had happened. But how? Their grandpa grabbed them both by the shoulders. Patrick was surprised at the strength of his grip.

"I . . . I don't know how you two got in here. . . ."

Becky dried a tear with the sleeve of her dress. "Grandpa, you scared us."

"I'm sorry, lass. I meant you no distress, but I . . . I've not been quite myself. . . . Something about this headache. D'you understand?"

Patrick knew he did not understand. Not at all. He didn't move, and neither did Becky.

"Not a word of this to your parents, now. Or to anyone else, for that matter."

Patrick was still too scared to even nod.

"I must have your word!" insisted the Old Man. He gripped Patrick's shoulder even more tightly.

"But why?" whispered Becky. "Why don't you want help?"

Finally the Old Man let go, and he pointed around him. "You see this vessel? She's almost alive, and I worked hard for her. She's all I have left of Elisabeth, your grandmother."

Patrick nodded. *Lady Elisabeth* was more than just a name.

His grandpa went on. "I worked hard for a place on the river. Only now they're talking about licenses and such. Master's certificates. Foolishness. But do you think they're going to let an old man like me stand for such a certificate? Not if they think he's as sick as I am, they won't. They'll find another younger man, give the certificate to *him*."

He pounded on the boiler of his steam engine to make his point.

"No, I've worked too hard and too long on this river to let it slip away just like that. . . ."

"Are you sick, Grandpa?" Becky asked softly. "You keep having headaches, do you not?"

He stiffened, as if he had said too much, then shook his head.

"It's nothing. Happened before you arrived. Just an accident. A bump on the head is all."

The Old Man again put his hands on their shoulders and guided them out into the night. Over his shoulder Patrick saw the sweat on his grandpa's forehead.

"Not a word to your parents," he told them. "*Especially* not to your parents."

Patrick didn't know how to promise that.

"Your word, now," insisted their grandpa. "Both of you."

"Only if you promise to go see Dr. Thompson when we get to Echuca," replied Becky.

Patrick didn't hear his grandpa agree, but he didn't say no, either. A minute later the steam engine began puffing once more, and Patrick listened to the *splash-splash* of the two pumps.

The Old Man had been right—at least about how long it would take to empty the *Lady Elisabeth* of all her water.

"You do the arithmetic," Luke told Patrick as they scrubbed mud from the deck two days later. Patrick looked up from his bucket and mop with a grin.

"Forty days and forty nights? I have no idea, Luke. You're the mathematical genius."

Luke sighed. "All right. It's simple, really. The *Lady E* is sixty feet long, twelve feet wide, about six feet deep. Filled with water. How much is that?"

Patrick didn't answer. He knew his aborigine friend would answer his own question. He had no idea how a boy from a mostly uninhabited island could be so smart.

"All right, I'll tell you—if she were a square bathtub, that would be over four thousand cubic feet...."

Patrick wasn't sure he even knew what a cubic foot was, but he let Luke continue.

"And with seven and a half gallons to a cubic foot, that's—"

"But how long to pump it out?" interrupted Patrick.

"I'm getting to that. I figure fifty hours. Two days, as long as the pumping doesn't stop."

"That's all I wanted to know." Patrick returned to his scrubbing. Over the side, his father was hammering on a more respectable patch of wood to replace the canvas.

"Once we get under way," he had told them, "we won't have much time to stop."

His sister and mother were already loading what supplies and tools they had as the paddle steamer floated higher and higher.

Only twenty-eight days before we have to be in Goolwa, Patrick reminded himself, *or all this work will be for nothing*.

"Have you ever made it down the river so quickly, Captain?" asked Luke as he finished scrubbing his part of the deck.

The Old Man scratched his chin and frowned. "It's been done."

But not without a crew, thought Patrick.

He continued to scrub, but something felt very different about the *Lady Elisabeth* when his father jumped on with a heavy box of tools from the wagon. He looked over at Luke.

"I felt it, too," Luke told him, guessing the question. They both looked over the side at the river below. One of the pumps was sputtering and spitting instead of putting out a steady stream of water. That could only mean . . .

"We're floating!" they yelled, almost in the same breath. Becky rushed over to them, a big smile on her face.

"We've been floating for almost an hour," she told them. "You haven't noticed before now?"

Patrick looked around to see the Old Man standing behind the wheel, looking ready to sail his muddy paddle steamer down the river.

"She still looks like an Arkansas hog after a good roll in the mud," said Jefferson. He stood on the bank with the horses. The one he and Luke had ridden to Boomerang Bend was tied behind the wagon, and he looked ready to leave, too.

"We'll fix that in due time," answered Mr. McWaid, tapping a hammer in the palm of his hand. "So, Jefferson, you'll meet us at the Echuca wharf, is that right?"

"Yes, sir." Jefferson nodded. "And I'll stop by the cabin to pick up your things, the way you said. I'm sure that will save us some time."

"Just tell Mr. Duggan we're obliged to him for letting us use the wagon . . . and that we're sorry it took so long to return."

Jefferson nodded, leaned over to tell Becky something, then flicked the reins and headed down a trail through the trees.

True, the *Lady Elisabeth* still needed a good scrub. Her once gleaming white paint had a distinct gray-brown tinge from being dipped in the river so long. And the Old Man could hardly see through the muddy front window of his wheelhouse, so he just hung out the side door.

But the twin smokestacks belched black smoke, and the twin paddle wheels—one on each side—churned the river into foam. The eager little boat tugged on her leash like a puppy ready for a walk.

"Let's not waste any more time here," bellowed the captain. "We'll pump the rest of the water as we go."

That was all Patrick needed to hear. After Becky and Mrs. McWaid checked the campsite and scrambled aboard, Luke and Patrick pulled in the planks and stowed them on deck.

"Looks like our patch is holding fine," said Mr. McWaid, peeking down inside the boat at the few inches of water that still sloshed around. Michael stood in the front of the bow with his koala on his shoulders, waving useless directions to his grandpa.

"I can see well enough, lad," called the Old Man. "We don't want you falling in again."

Patrick shuddered at the thought as they steamed away from Boomerang Bend. His grandpa sounded the whistle—long and loud—as Mr. McWaid disappeared inside the boat to tend the engine and their mother set to cleaning up the inside.

"We'll make it in time," Luke told him, and Patrick nodded. The spring air felt good on his face, fresh and full of the scents of the river. He breathed in deeply, then noticed his sister staring off at the trees in the direction Jefferson had disappeared.

"What was he talking to you about when he was leaving?" asked Patrick, remembering how Jefferson had whispered to his sister.

Becky crossed her arms as they rounded the first of many turns and bends on their way back downriver. She did not look at all happy.

"He said he's going to look for Warburton in Echuca when he gets there." Patrick could barely hear his sister's voice over the slapping and splashing of the paddle wheels.

"Oh no." Patrick groaned quietly and closed his eyes. He couldn't imagine what Jeff would do, even if he found the man. Challenge him to a fight? Grab the money and run? After all they had been through since their trip from Ireland, Patrick wasn't sure he wanted to have anything to do with another adventure like that. He tried not to look at his sister and watched the trees go by as they raced down the flooded river.

They came to a stretch where the river had washed over its banks, and the narrow strip of eucalyptus was knee deep in muddy water for several hundred yards on either side.

"Hard to tell where the land stops," Patrick thought out loud. His sister didn't answer. Up ahead, a couple of the tallest trees on that stretch of the river marked yet another turn. Even with the flooding, they couldn't just cut off the corners of the winding river. But the *Lady Elisabeth* steamed on, straight for the trees.

He'd better turn pretty soon. Patrick looked at the tree and back at his grandpa, who gripped the big wooden steering wheel with white knuckles.

"Grandpa?" Becky noticed it, too. Up behind the wheel, their grandpa shook his head, then held the side of his face in obvious pain. The paddle wheels kept turning as they raced straight for the trees.

Becky was two steps closer to her grandpa than Patrick, but it did her no good. Neither would be able to reach the Old Man in time.

"Grandpa!" screamed Becky as she raced for him.

Patrick tried to climb the step ladder from the main deck to the wheelhouse, but that turned out to be a mistake. A branch caught Patrick in the face as they brushed by the trees, sweeping him off the ladder and dumping him on the deck below.

CHAPTER 7

GOLD RUSH

"Patrick?" Mr. McWaid saw him as he fell to the deck and landed on his back.

Patrick gasped for breath but could not find it; all he could do was squirm in pain. His father kneeled next to him, but the voice sounded far away, as if Mr. McWaid were talking through a tube.

"Patrick?" It felt to Patrick as if the man hovering over him was sitting on his chest.

"That—" Patrick finally managed to pull in a little gasp of air, just enough to squeak. "That hurt."

"Don't talk," his father commanded him. Patrick nodded and worked at catching his breath.

"Are you all right, boy?" His grandpa leaned out the window and glanced down at them. "That riverbank was a little closer than I reckoned."

Patrick looked at his sister, who shrugged her shoulders from behind the Old Man.

"Looks like the trees nearly took out a searchlight here on deck." Their father pointed to a kerosene lamp mounted on the railing next to the wheelhouse, nearly bent off its mounting bracket.

"Hmm." The Old Man nodded and pulled the lamp back into place before he returned his attention to the river ahead of them.

They were back in the middle of the Murray, back on course for Echuca. Patrick looked at the trees they had clipped and the pile of branches that had fallen onto the deck.

"Perfect!" Michael hopped out on deck and picked up a handful of leaves. "This is the kind of leaf Christopher likes best. Thanks, Grandpa!"

"I picked them just for you," mumbled Patrick, and his father helped him to his feet.

"Well, son," his father told Patrick, "you're a little scratched up. But apparently you're still in working order."

Patrick finally took a deep breath. "I'll have to be more careful."

Racing downriver on the dark, swollen Murray, the Old Man told them he thought they could cut a good hour off their normal time to Echuca. Still, it was nearly dark before they approached the lights of the little river port. In the meantime Patrick's parents had been talking quietly on the rear deck, enjoying the soft evening air. In the distance they could hear the faint howling of a pair of dingoes, Australia's wild dogs. Luke had been dozing in the main salon, near Michael, who was curled up on a mat with his koala. Becky continued washing down musty-smelling cabinets in the galley.

"Ooh," she said, opening up a rusty round tin and sniffing. "This was once flour."

"You're sure we can't save it?" Patrick teased her as she stepped over to the deck and dumped the contents overboard. He noticed that she glanced up to check on the Old Man in the wheelhouse just above them.

"Do you think one of us is going to have to stay with him from now on?" wondered Patrick.

Becky shook her head and lowered her voice. "We don't want to crash into the trees again, do we?"

"No. That was too close. What do you think is wrong with him?"

"I don't know. But maybe Dr. Thompson will be able to tell us.

As soon as we tie up, I'm going to see if he'll come down to the wharf."

"Right," agreed Patrick. "It's a sure thing the captain won't go up to see *him*."

By that time they could make out a few more lights on the shore—most from the windows of riverfront warehouses.

"Everyone on deck!" shouted the Old Man, thumping his heel on the deck. "Echuca!"

Of course, they already knew well the riverfront town spread out before them. Their stopping place was the tall wooden pier built by the government to help turn Echuca into the "Chicago of the West." They would probably be the smallest of some six paddle steamers there. Two or three, like the *Lady Elisabeth*, looked like general cargo carriers, the workhorses of the Murray River. A couple of barges were tied up, too, the ones used for carrying wool from outlying ranches called sheep stations. Next to them floated an impressive white passenger steamer, three decks tall and maybe three times the length of the little *Lady E*.

"What we lack in size," their grandpa had once told them, "we make up for in spirit."

He wasn't talking tonight, though, as he eased his vessel into an open spot. As soon as they were close enough, Patrick leaped off with one of the lines they would use to tie up with. He planted his heels and held on as their momentum threatened to take them into the passenger boat just ahead.

"I've got it." Patrick grunted but held on, and he looked quickly around the wharf.

"Where is everyone?" he asked Becky, who snubbed the other line by wrapping it a few times around one of the wharf's big round pilings. She glanced around with a puzzled look, barely visible in the light from a lantern that hung nearby. Patrick jumped when he heard a whoop and a shot just up the street in one of the taverns.

"Does that answer your question?" Becky asked him. She tied the line fast with a couple of expert twists. Patrick made a mental note to ask her sometime how to do that knot.

"Sure," answered Patrick. "But there's usually *someone* on the wharf."

They all stood on the wharf next to the *Lady Elisabeth* for a minute after Mr. McWaid shut down the steam engine. Even the Old Man looked worried.

"I can hear 'em carrying on up there in town." The Old Man put his two fingers in his mouth and whistled, then cupped his hands to his mouth and shouted.

"G. P. Fisher! Ervin! Say, you fellows there?"

Patrick recognized the names of men who worked at the wharf, operating the cranes that helped load and unload the endless cargoes from up and down the river and the farms that lined the valley.

"Where *are* those boys?" wondered the Old Man when a dark shape slipped around the corner of the nearest brick warehouse.

"You there!" shouted the Old Man. "Have you seen G. P.? I just pulled in, and—"

"G. P.'s gone," said the man. He was their father's age, judging from the sound of his voice, and a little unsteady on his feet. He started to walk past them until the Old Man jumped down and stopped him.

"Wait a minute. What about Ervin Johnson? I need to get some supplies loaded in a hurry."

"Ervin's gone, too."

The Old Man didn't let go of the man's arm. "Wherever would he go to? He still works here, does he not?"

The man shook his head. "No, sir. He's gone to the gold field, like just about everyone else in Echuca. All that's left are the women and children."

"What?" Now Patrick's father stepped up. "What gold?"

Finally the man turned to study them. When he grinned it was obvious several of his front teeth were missing.

"I thought everybody knew by now. Fella by the name of Miller found a pretty good-sized nugget in one of the creeks just a couple of miles up the Campaspe River about two days ago. Could be as big as the Bendigo gold strike, is what I hear. That's where I'm headed."

"Miller?" The Old Man's eyes widened. "Why, I wouldn't trust him farther than I could toss a two-pound Murray codfish. Doesn't he own a lot of useless billabongs up there he's been trying to sell? Marshland, floods every year. Probably underwater even as we speak."

"You see the nugget, sir, you might change your mind."

"A fool's gold." The Old Man cleared his throat in disgust, pushed past the stranger, and stomped across the wharf toward the celebration.

"I'm going to find me some supplies around here," he grumbled, "if I have to open up the shops myself."

"Wait a minute," their father called after him. "I'll be needing to speak with Mr. Field at the newspaper office."

The Old Man hardly slowed as Mr. McWaid trotted after him. After their grandpa had left, Michael turned to his older sister.

"Did they really find gold?"

Becky shrugged and checked the mooring lines. "People have been talking about finding gold on the Murray Flat for a long time. I suppose it could be."

Another shot went off in town; this time it sounded as if someone was starting a horse race down Conolly Street, off to the right. Their mother shuddered and pulled Patrick and Becky back to the boat.

"All the same," she told them, "I'll be glad to be on our way. It sounds as if this gold thing has whipped people up."

Becky stood her ground and stared at the town. "But I thought Jeff was going to be here to meet us."

Patrick had almost forgotten. "Maybe he went off to find himself some gold."

Instead of smiling, Becky looked back at him with a first-class frown. Luke scanned the town, too, without smiling.

"Sorry," mumbled Patrick, stepping back on the *Lady Elisabeth* to wait. "It was just a joke."

By the time their father and the Old Man returned two hours later, even Patrick was beginning to wonder about Jefferson.

"Did you see Mr. Mullarky?" asked Becky. Her grandpa handed across a box full of groceries, a bag of flour, and more sugar. He was loaded down with two more, high above his head.

"I did," replied the Old Man, "and did I give him a piece of my mind. His shop was already closed, and it's only ten o'clock! And then he has the nerve to tell me I have to pay cash, on account of his being nearly cleaned out by all these crazy fellows with gold fever. 'I'm sorry, sir, I can't put it on your account any longer,' he tells me. I've never heard of such a thing!"

"What about Jefferson?" Patrick took one of the other boxes and followed his sister into the galley.

"What?" The Old Man set down his load.

"Jefferson Pitney," Patrick repeated. "He was going to meet us here at the wharf. We all figured he would arrive ahead of us."

"Oh yes." The Old Man handed Patrick a brown paper sack of sugar. "Well, maybe he got caught up in a bit of gold—"

"Don't say it," warned their mother.

"We *did* tell him to meet us here," the Old Man wondered out loud. "Didn't we?"

Mr. McWaid nodded quietly, and Patrick could tell from the stormy expression on his face that something was wrong. His father disappeared into the boat, Mrs. McWaid on his heels.

"Dear, did you talk to Mr. Field at the newspaper about work?"

"What work?" Mr. McWaid's voice came straight through the cabin. "There is no work."

Patrick looked down at the deck, feeling as if he was listening in on a private conversation. But like everyone else, he couldn't help hearing. The Old Man turned away and coiled up a rope to look busy. Luke started rolling out his bedroll on top of the main cabin. Becky strolled off the rear deck, but the voices followed them.

"What do you mean, no work?" asked their mother.

"Just that," continued their father. "The fellow who had my job before, well, he came back while we were gone. And Field gave him his job back."

"But he can't do that!" protested Mrs. McWaid. "What are we going to do now?"

"It's done, Sarah, and maybe it's for the best. 'Twas a temporary reporting job, remember? Just a little more temporary than I'd hoped."

The voices of Patrick's parents finally blended into the night sounds of the river and the town. On the other side of the river, it sounded as if bullfrogs had taken over the swampy little town of Moama—Echuca's twin city. And every once in a while, his parents' words floated out, too.

"What about your father's money?" wondered Mrs. McWaid.

"He's still a bit confused about that part . . ." replied Mr. McWaid, and then something about "And the constable wasn't much help."

As the night wore on, Becky started pacing up and down the deck of the *Lady E*; she didn't give up until nearly midnight. The Old Man slept up in the wheelhouse, although his mattress—along with just about everything else on the boat that wasn't tied down or in a drawer—must have floated away when the *Lady Elisabeth* sank.

Finally Patrick's parents fell asleep, too, or at least their feeble oil lamp was blown out. Michael and his koala were tucked away. Even Luke lay quietly in his corner of the deck, outside as always. Only Patrick couldn't sleep, wondering where his friend had disappeared to.

It's not like him, he thought. *If Jeff said he was going to meet us, then something has to be wrong.*

Patrick sat on the wharf side of the deck, his legs dangling over the side, listening to water sounds and the occasional dog howling up in town. The lantern on the wharf had long since burned dry, but there was enough light from the mild spring evening to make out the dark outlines of the other paddle steamers there.

I'll just rest my eyes for a minute, he finally told himself and pulled in his legs. He didn't remember anything else until he felt a hand on his shoulder.

"What?" Patrick jerked awake and nearly toppled into the river. The grip on his shoulder tightened, and he felt a hand on his mouth.

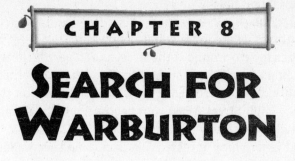

CHAPTER 8

SEARCH FOR WARBURTON

"No sense waking everyone up," whispered the person in the dark. The distinct southern drawl told Patrick all he needed to know.

"Jeff," he whispered after his friend slowly lifted his hand away. "We all thought you—"

"Never mind that," Jefferson interrupted. "Just follow me."

"No, wait." Patrick looked around at the dark shape of the *Lady Elisabeth* and shivered for the first time all night. But when he turned back, Jefferson was gone.

"Jefferson!" hissed Patrick, not loud enough, he hoped, to wake anyone on the boat. He scrambled around a tall pile of wooden crates to find his friend waiting for him under a flickering lantern hung against the wall of a warehouse.

"Where have you *been*?" asked Patrick. "We were starting to think you'd gone off to find gold."

"What?" laughed Jefferson. "Like the rest of the town? Not me."

"So what took you so long?"

Jefferson looked around the shadowy waterfront as if he were about to tell a secret. "Took me a little longer to get to town than I thought. Had to go around a few swamps that were flooded over."

"All right, but what are we doing here?"

"Oh, well, don't you want to find Warburton and get your grandpa's money back?"

"Sure, but—"

"So this is where we're going to find him."

Patrick looked around at the street and shivered. The whooping and singing around them made it hard to hear each other.

"Hey, kid," called someone from the door of one of the hotels that lined High Street. "Past your bedtime, don't you think?"

Patrick didn't know how to answer.

"Just ignore him," ordered Jefferson, "and keep walking."

Patrick followed Jeff as they doubled back around one of the hotels to the rear entry. He jumped when a couple of scruffy-looking wild dogs came racing between their legs. One clutched a half-chewed bone tightly in its teeth, and the other had just managed to grab a corner of the prize and hang on.

"Just follow what I do," the tall American told Patrick. A pair of rusty hinges screeched as Jeff pulled open the back door. They stepped into a crowded kitchen filled with steam and the smell of dirty dishes. Black skillets and huge iron kettles hung from a rack in the middle of the room, and tables around the edges were piled high with greasy plates, cups, and saucers of every size. In the middle of it all sat a skinny-looking young man wearing a smudged apron and a tired expression. He was surrounded by a pile of pots, pans, and dishes almost as tall as himself.

"Hey, Arthur!" Jefferson greeted the cook with a wave. The young man smiled back.

"The crazy Yank!" He tossed a tin cup into a huge bowl of soapy water in front of him. "Haven't seen you in weeks. You haven't come by for a free lunch lately."

Jeff returned the smile. "We've been helping Patrick's grandpa raise the *Lady Elisabeth*. Arthur, I want you to meet a friend of mine, Patrick McWaid."

Arthur's expression changed as if he had been hit by lightning. Instead of taking Patrick's outstretched hand, he returned to his dishes.

"Did I say something wrong?" asked Jeff. "We just came by to say howdy."

"Yeh, well, you'd better leave before my boss sees you here," mumbled Arthur. "I'm not supposed to have anybody back here."

Patrick put his hand in his pocket and backed toward the door. "Look, Jeff, it's all right. Maybe we'd best return to the boat."

But Jefferson didn't move. "Not until I find out what's going on."

"Look, Jeff, I don't want to be rude, but you've got to go." The young cook looked up and mopped the sweat off his forehead with the sleeve of his white shirt. "People have been talking about what happened up at Boomerang Bend while the Old Man was trying to raise his paddle steamer."

Jefferson looked at Patrick. "Do you know what he's talking about?"

Patrick was almost afraid to answer, but of course he knew.

"People got hurt up there," continued the cook. "Crew came through and disappeared. People on the river are talking about a jinx on the *Lady Elisabeth*."

Jefferson laughed. "Oh, is that all? I thought you were serious."

Arthur shook his head. "All I know is what I heard from the fellows who came back. They were pretty shaken up."

"Pretty shook up, until the gold fever struck." Jefferson shook his head. "I can't believe you people would just swallow all the rubbish Warburton told you."

Arthur stopped scrubbing a pan and bit his lip but didn't look up.

"That's it, isn't it? Warburton comes through, and he tells everyone the *Lady Elisabeth* is unlucky. That the Old Man was going to kill his entire crew, right?"

"You'd better go, Jeff. I don't want you to get into trouble. That bloke still has friends around here. He's even pretty good mates with my boss, which is why . . ."

By that time Patrick was at the door, trying to push his way out, but Jefferson held his arm.

"Oh, I see. Your boss thinks Mr. Warburton is a great customer and wants to see him back, is that it?"

Arthur didn't answer, didn't look up.

"He did have a big pile of money, didn't he?"

The cook looked down.

"Come on, answer me!"

Arthur finally nodded. "Said he inherited it. . . ."

Jefferson almost laughed. "More like *stole* it from the Old Man. That money was for . . ." His voice trailed off, then he waved his hand. "Aw, never mind. It's not your fault. Thanks, Art."

Patrick looked at the cook and nodded. "Nice to meet you."

That was a silly thing to say, he told himself. Arthur didn't answer, and Jefferson stopped in the doorway but didn't turn around.

"One more thing, Arthur," said Jefferson. "You don't happen to know if Warburton left town yet, do you?"

"Two days ago, I think. Just before we heard about the gold."

"Downriver?"

Patrick saw the man nod.

"Know which boat?"

"No. Listen, Jefferson. I—"

"All right, all right." Jefferson stepped back out into the dark of the alley. "We found out what we need to know. Thanks."

Patrick thought he heard the cook sigh with relief as the door slammed behind them. One last look told him the fellow had returned to his dishes in earnest. Out in the alley the dogs were still battling for their bone.

"Just what I thought," said Jefferson. "Mr. Warburton leaves your grandpa to rot, has a little fun in Echuca, and heads down the river. He'll have the loot all spent before he makes Adelaide—if we don't stop him first."

"Stop him?" croaked Patrick. His throat felt dry.

Jefferson narrowed his eyes at Patrick as they passed through the half-lit streets. "What else? He has to be on that big passenger steamer, the *Gem*. All we have to do is catch up to it."

"I don't know, I . . ." After Jefferson's performance in the hotel kitchen, Patrick didn't doubt for a moment that he was serious.

Patrick would have slept later the next morning, except that his father woke him up with a slam of the door as he stepped back aboard the paddle steamer.

"Where are you going, Pa?" Patrick asked quietly, wiping the sleep out of his eyes. It seemed like just minutes ago that Jefferson had been dragging him around the streets of Echuca.

"Going? We're loading up, my boy!" boomed his father, much too loudly, it seemed, for that time of the morning. But off in the engine room Patrick heard the distinct crackle of firewood heating up the boiler and the huff of first steam.

"Oh, does that mean Jefferson arrived with the rest of our things last night?" asked their mother.

Jefferson answered the question by jumping down to the paddle steamer with a box in his arms.

"These your kitchen things, Ms. McWaid?" he asked, bowing and holding out the box.

"I was needing this!" Patrick's mother glanced into the box and pulled out a wooden pancake turner.

"Sorry I was delayed," Jefferson apologized. "But I was able to stop by the cabin and gather up all the rest of your things."

"Thank you, Jefferson." Patrick's father took the box. "Sounds as if we're right on time. You didn't forget . . ."

"No, no, the rest of the books are aboard." Jefferson ruffled Michael's already-messy hair as he stumbled out on deck to see what was going on. "Sorry, Michael, but if you're not going to be able to go to school, school is going to come to you. And Patrick and Becky, too."

"Ma," Michael yawned, "is that true?"

Mrs. McWaid crossed her arms and smiled at her three children. "I know you've had your reader with you. But this time your father and I decided that if we're all going to stay together, you're surely going to keep up with your book learning. That means *all* your books."

"I thought we were just going to learn from the river."

Their mother laughed. "Perhaps you'll do some of that, as—"

Just then their grandpa let loose with a brief blast of the steam whistle, just enough to let the town know they were leaving. A shrill steam whistle echoed across the river, then seemed to dance and echo around the wharf. A man unloading a wagon paused to watch. Echuca was not yet awake.

"With all this gold foolishness," complained the Old Man, hustling down the ladder from upstairs to check on the steam engine himself, "all the other paddle steamers can't get crews, either. Everyone jumped ship to find a fortune that's not there."

"We're all you've got now, Captain," said Mr. McWaid. His face was already smeared with oil.

For a moment everyone looked at the Old Man. Becky and her mother were in the galley, stacking the rest of the kitchen things. Patrick was about to hand his father a piece of split firewood, and Luke and Jefferson leaned in from the side deck, ready to let go the lines. Even Michael paused from feeding Christopher his breakfast. The captain of the *Lady Elisabeth* looked around, aware of everyone's eyes on him.

"Yes, well, I'm grateful for what crew I do have, that I am." He cleared his throat. "We'll just try to make it on time to Goolwa as best we can. Twenty-seven days. If we don't make it on time to save our half of the vessel, well, then, we'll make a good go of it."

"Say the word, Captain." Jefferson saluted smartly. "Shall I take the first watch on the barge?"

The Old Man nodded. "We'll need your sea experience, boy. I'm a bit concerned that it's overloaded. Keep it to the middle of the channel."

"Aye, aye!" Jefferson bounded up the ladder next to their boat and disappeared from view.

"Barge?" wondered Michael.

Their grandpa answered with a nod toward their stern, the back end of the paddle steamer, where a wide, flat barge loaded high with packed bales of wool had been pulled into place behind them. The load towered almost as high as the top deck of the *Lady Elisabeth*.

"Have to pay for the trip somehow," explained the Old Man.

"Good for us there weren't any other paddle steamers ready to leave town right away. Floods have covered some of the railway tracks, so we're taking this wool downriver ourselves. Aside from a wee hole in the side of the boat and a good layer of Murray River mud, we're more than ready to go."

Patrick looked back and up to see a pair of feet swing out from the wharf's loading crane, and Jefferson landed like an acrobat with a tumble on the barge's top bale of wool before taking up his position on the top of the bales, where a matching steering wheel had been set up. The wheel was almost as big around as Jeff was tall.

"See there." Mr. McWaid pointed out the window to show Michael. "He and Luke are going to steer the barge as we drag it along behind. They'll take turns keeping it in the river's deepest center."

"And me?" Michael looked hopeful.

Mr. McWaid laughed. "No, no, Michael. You'll do well to help your mother as she needs. Patrick and Becky are deck hands. Perhaps you could fetch wood on occasion."

"I could steer," insisted Michael. "I really could."

His father touched a greasy finger to Michael's nose with a smile and turned back to the steam engine. "I might need your help to keep this cranky old steam engine alive, so don't go far. We'll need all the hands we can get and every penny we can make to get down this river."

"But I don't have any money, Pa."

"No matter, boy. You just do what you can. We're all doing what we can to help your grandfather keep his paddle steamer."

Patrick watched them from a distance, joking and chatting, then helped his sister with the mooring lines as they eased away from the towering Echuca wharf. He coiled the lines into a circle on the deck as he had seen his grandpa do, then looked around again at the river scenery.

Here we go again, he thought, relaxing for the first time all morning. He could smell the breakfast of bread, jam, and boiled eggs his mother and Becky were fixing. And up in the wheelhouse of the *Lady Elisabeth*, the Old Man looked the same as Patrick had always remembered him: tall, straight-backed, and steely-eyed. In command, as usual. Until the Old Man held the side of his head and grimaced in pain.

"You know what we didn't do in Echuca, Becky?" Patrick asked his sister when she handed him a plate. He reached for the egg but missed when the *Lady Elisabeth* lurched wildly forward. Becky tumbled to the deck.

"Hold on!" shouted the Old Man from his perch up in the wheelhouse.

CHAPTER 9

RIVER ATTACK

"What on earth?" cried Becky. At any other time Patrick might have laughed at how she looked, lying on her back with a plate lifted high in the air, perfectly balanced. But he thought it was a better idea to help her quickly to her feet while the Old Man shouted instructions from his perch.

"Pull up the tow rope, would you, boy?"

Patrick sprang into action as their paddles furiously churned in reverse.

"Looks like we already broke the towline," Patrick said as he pulled the thick, wet line back up on deck. It reminded him of a big, angry snake.

"Why are we going backward?" asked Michael, rushing out on deck.

"Something broke," explained Patrick, reaching the end of the line. How it had broken, he couldn't say, but by that time the barge was drifting sideways behind them.

"Look at this!" shouted Jefferson as they closed in on the barge and bumped gently together. He held up a twisted piece of metal, the cleat they had obviously tied the rope to earlier. "Pulled right out of the deck."

"Forget the deck hardware," hollered the Old Man. "Use the

71

post there on the deck. Tie it all the way around. I knew this barge was trouble from the start."

Patrick obeyed, jumping lightly to the forward deck of the barge with an armload of coiled rope. He quickly looped the rope five or six turns around the thickest post he could find, pulled back with all his weight, then secured it with two sailor knots Jefferson had once taught him.

"That's it." Jefferson nodded his approval. "Just the way we do it at sea."

"We should've done that in the first place," put in Luke, who was watching the wheel.

"Should've done that in the first place," echoed the Old Man. "I'm not going to ask who tied the barge up to begin with, but I'm hoping it wasn't one of you. Now, get back aboard, Patrick, and we'll be off again."

"See you, sailor." Jefferson winked at Patrick as he hopped back. "Didn't I tell you once that learning those knots would come in handy?"

Patrick smiled as the rope tightened and they made their way down the Murray.

"Your turn to watch Grandpa," Becky whispered in his ear as he passed her, back on the deck of the *Lady Elisabeth*. "We have to keep an eye on him, make sure he's all right."

Patrick sighed but nodded and climbed up to stand on the upper deck. The Old Man pretended not to notice him. He just muttered that it was a wonder the barge wasn't underwater.

"It's probably that jinx," muttered the Old Man, "coming back to bite me." He kept his eyes on the twisting river ahead as they moved back into the current.

After their first week on the river, Patrick was used to the routine. From up in the wheelhouse one day, he listened to the swish of the paddle wheels and counted squat kookaburras looking for fish from their perches high above the river. They were his favorite, the laughing symbol of the Australian bush. The Old Man broke into his thoughts.

"Hoping to steer again, are you?"

Is that why he thinks I'm here? Patrick wondered.

"No, sir." Patrick shook his head, perhaps overdoing it. "Last time I steered I . . . uh . . . well, you remember what happened." Patrick could still remember the sickening sound of the log that had punched a hole through the side of the paddle steamer.

And it was all my fault, Patrick told himself, the same way he had told himself a hundred times before, ever since the *Lady Elisabeth* went down.

"I remember well enough," said the Old Man flatly. His face didn't show whatever he was thinking, though Patrick searched for a clue. "You'll get over it, I expect. We'll teach you to be a riverman yet."

I'll get over it? wondered Patrick, sure that he wouldn't. He stayed outside the wheelhouse at a safe distance, keeping an eye on his grandpa out of the corner of his eye.

They still had not caught up with the *Gem*, the paddle steamer Jefferson thought Warburton had taken. And they had only twenty-two days to get to Goolwa.

"Patrick!" called the Old Man, and Patrick jumped at the sudden sound of his grandpa's voice. The Old Man motioned him inside and pointed to the river chart.

"You might as well learn something," mumbled the Old Man, pointing to the scroll. "Tell me where we are."

Patrick looked closely at the snaking outline of the Murray River chart and tried to make out some of the details that had been scratched on and penciled in.

"There, see that old marker tree?" The Old Man pointed at a gnarled tree hanging over the bank. Patrick noted a little drawing of a tree on the chart. "Aborigines probably have a name for that tree, it's been around so long."

Up ahead the Old Man pointed out a sunken boat, which the chart showed as a drawing of a wreck.

"That's been there as long as I can remember, too," remarked the Old Man. "Only it keeps rolling down the river a little more each year. Now, where are we?"

Patrick looked up and down the river and rechecked the chart. The shadows were getting much longer, and the sunset was putting on a show of orange and yellow in the west. Up ahead, he thought he could see a small boat with a couple of fishermen.

"Getting closer to Swan Hill?" he guessed.

"That's right." The Old Man nodded and pointed ahead of them. "Be there by full dark. And you see that . . ." His voice trailed off, and he squeezed his eyes shut as they paddled on.

Meanwhile, the fishermen were getting much closer. One of them looked up at the paddle steamer coming their way.

"Um . . ." Patrick wondered if he should say something, but his grandpa was rubbing his eyes and forehead. They seemed to be steaming even faster toward the little craft in their path, and now both fishermen were staring straight at them and waving.

"Do you see those fisher—"

"Of course I see them!" thundered the Old Man. He gritted his teeth and stared straight ahead, shaking his head all the while. Patrick could see his grandpa swallow hard, then he looked back at the barge. Luke was steering and could also see what was happening. He waved his hands wildly.

We're going to run right over them, thought Patrick, but there was nothing he could do. One of the men on the fishing boat struggled with putting his oars in place while the other pulled in their lines, hand over hand.

"Grandpa?" shouted Becky from the side deck. "Do you see the boat?" She was frozen in place, watching the river ahead.

"I . . . see . . . them," whispered the Old Man, squinting and swinging the wheel uncertainly from side to side.

Patrick thought afterward that he probably should have grabbed the wheel. But that was afterward, and at the moment of the crash he couldn't take his eyes off the boat ahead of them. The two men gave up on their fishing lines and jumped overboard, one to the right and the other to the left. The *Lady Elisabeth* might have cleared the rowboat, but something lodged in her portside paddle wheel.

"Pa!" Patrick finally found his voice. "We've got to stop! Stop the engine!"

Becky passed along the message. The fishing boat banged against the side of their boat and turned over.

Patrick was the first to reach the side where the boat had overturned. He grabbed a long pole with a knobby hook on the end, hooked it over the side of the boat, and held fast.

"Becky!" he cried. "Give me a hand."

But by that time she had already thrown out a rope over the other side of the boat to rescue one of the red-faced fishermen. With their father up on deck, they hauled the two dripping, sputtering men to safety. Patrick tied the rowboat, which was full of water, to their side. He tried to get out of the way when the largest of the two came charging toward the wheelhouse, but he wasn't quick enough.

"Out of my way!" growled the man, shaking the water off his long black beard. "Who's the fool who ran us over?"

He pushed Patrick to the side on his way up, and murder flashed in his eyes.

"See here," objected the Old Man. "It was all an accident."

But the man didn't stop.

"It was no accident," growled the big man, still climbing.

Patrick didn't stop to think and grabbed at the back of the man's shirt as he climbed up the ladder.

"Shove off!" roared the attacker. He swung his fist wildly, grazing Patrick's ear. But Patrick ducked, got a better grip, and held on.

"You leave my grandfather alone!" yelled Patrick, digging his fingers into the man's back. The move proved to be a mistake as the man's elbow connected squarely with Patrick's jaw, and his head spun in shock.

CHAPTER 10

UNWELCOME OFFER

"I said get off!" The man tumbled to the deck, carrying Patrick with him. But even with his head still swimming, Patrick held on.

"No!" Patrick shouted back. He rode the man as far as he could, grabbing around his shoulders and neck. "It really *was* an accident!"

By then the Old Man had come down on his own, where he joined the brawl. The big fisherman was still roaring like a bear and trying to swing at anyone he could reach. Mr. McWaid slipped around behind and pried Patrick away before grabbing the man's arms. In the meantime, the other fisherman stood off to the side with his hands in the air. He was a small, plump man with a wide-brimmed hat and a sunburned nose, and his eyes were wide with either excitement or fright.

"Wes!" he cried. "Wes, it's just a boy. Stop it, Wesley!"

Wesley the bear-man finally stopped long enough to breathe, but Patrick was afraid the man had not yet given up the fight.

"That's enough," ordered Mr. McWaid, trying to get a better grip on the man's elbows. Patrick knew his father would have a hard time hanging on if the big fellow decided to explode again. Mrs. McWaid came out with a broom in her hand, ready to use it.

"He's fine," said the plump man as he rushed over to help his friend. "Aren't you, Wesley?"

Wesley easily broke free of Mr. McWaid's grip, his lip curling as he turned to face the Old Man. Patrick prepared to launch into him again, but his father held up his hand.

"Now, listen here," he commanded, and the sound of his voice made even Wesley stop and take notice. "We've had a little accident, but it looks like no one is hurt. There's no need to be angry."

"But he—" Wesley blustered, pointing a huge, meaty hand at Patrick's grandpa. "He ran us over . . . deliberately."

The way the fellow said "deliberately" sounded as if he had practiced it over and over again, like a kid facing the hardest word on a spelling test.

"No, no, Wesley." The little man stepped up and patted his friend's arm. Patrick noticed a tattoo of a parrot flying on one of Wesley's bulging muscles. "I'm sure these people meant us no harm. Look, our boat is fine. We'll just need a little drying out, is all."

"That's right," said Mrs. McWaid. "It was an accident. Why don't you two gentlemen come inside to dry off, and we'll feed you some soup."

The big man seemed to take a breath for the first time, and he looked slowly around at everyone.

"What kind of soup?" he asked, turning his attention away from the relieved Old Man.

"A nice, hot fish chowder," she told them all. "Plenty for everyone, right, John?"

Mrs. McWaid bit her lip and glanced at her husband, who nodded. She smiled, but Patrick noticed she had knotted her apron in her hands.

"There, you see, Wesley?" The man shook the river water out of his ear. "This is really our lucky day, after all. What was I going to fix you for supper?"

Wesley shrugged as he backed away from the Old Man and followed the others into the *Lady Elisabeth*'s salon. Over on the barge, Jefferson and Luke stared helplessly.

"What's going on over there?" yelled Jefferson.

Mr. McWaid waved back as the barge drifted closer. "We're all right, boys."

"I was ready to swim over and help, Mr. McWaid," volunteered Jefferson. "And if I knew how to swim, that's what I surely would have done."

Mr. McWaid laughed. "I'm sure you would have, lad. Good thing we didn't need your assistance."

Back in the galley, Mrs. McWaid went right to work chopping up extra fish and throwing a few more onions into her steaming chowder. A few minutes later there really *was* enough for everyone.

"Ah, perfect." The shorter of their two guests leaned over the soup kettle and breathed in the steam. "We'd be very pleased to share your supper, seeing as how Wesley and I weren't having much luck fishing for ourselves." He tucked a napkin under his chin, took the first bowl offered, and was just about to dive in with his spoon when Mr. McWaid cleared his throat.

"Ah, excuse me, Mr., ah . . ."

"Hamilton." The man smiled and the name rolled off his tongue as if he had introduced royalty. "Adam Hamilton, at your service."

"Yes, well, Mr. Hamilton." Patrick's father sat with his hands in his lap. "We normally give thanks for our food."

Mr. Hamilton dropped his spoon in mid-slurp but kept a smile on his face.

"Yes, of course, by all means," agreed their guest, and he bowed his head quickly for the prayer before everyone else joined him in devouring the chowder.

"Do you want to take this bowl up to Grandpa with me?" Becky whispered to Patrick when Wesley and Hamilton took to their bowls as if they hadn't eaten in weeks. Patrick nodded, not sure that he wanted to talk to his grandpa yet but very sure that he didn't want to share any more soup with the odd couple they had plucked out of the river. Becky balanced a large mug of steaming chowder, and Patrick led the way up the ladder to the wheelhouse.

"Thank you." The Old Man never took his eyes off the darkening river ahead as he reached for the mug in Becky's hand. Patrick fidgeted by the door, one foot in and one foot out.

"Are you coming or going?" the Old Man finally asked with only the hint of a sideways glance. "Best be comin'. I've something to say to the both of you."

But when the Old Man reached for the soup, his hand was not where Becky's was. She nearly dropped it before she tried to give it to him again. Finally they connected, and the Old Man squeezed his eyes shut as he took a sip.

"There, you see?" he finally breathed. "This is directly what I'm of a mind to tell you, but I'll need your word again that nothing I say goes beyond the three of us."

"We haven't told anyone, Grandpa," whispered Becky. The Old Man blew on the chowder and took a careful sip.

"Well, then," continued their grandpa, "it seems me eyes, they aren't working as well as they used to. And I was thinking . . ."

"Is that why we ran over the fishermen?" Patrick blurted out, and instantly he wanted to bite his tongue. His grandpa seemed to hide behind the steam rising out of his chowder mug.

"Yes, well, actually, I did have a bit of trouble. . . ."

Up ahead of them, the dim lights from the river town of Swan Hill twinkled softly. Patrick wished once more he had kept his mouth shut.

The Old Man sighed. "Truth be told, I'm feeling as blind as a bat lately."

"Your headaches?" wondered Becky.

"Ah, maybe that's part of it, lass, I don't know. But I'm seeing two or three of everything more often than not, and it's getting a touch exasperating."

He held up one finger in front of his face.

"Two fingers I see here, and two of each of you, a-waverin' about like ghosts. Same way as I was seeing two of that blasted fishing boat. Here I was, staring down at the river, commanding my eyes to see properly, and they would not. Worse yet, I couldn't decide soon enough which fishing boat was the real one, and which was the ghost."

"But, Grandpa." Becky touched her grandpa's shoulder. "That's why we wanted you to see a doctor back in Echuca. Perhaps he could have—"

"No!" he insisted. "That's not a point we're debating. I've already told you what would happen. What I need now from the both of you is your eyes. I'm going to teach you to steer this river properly, if it be the last thing I do in this life!"

Patrick shivered at the thought.

"Both of us?" wondered Becky.

"Both of you." The Old Man sounded sure of himself now.

"So when do you want us to start?" asked Patrick. His voice was almost a whisper, like the warm spring breeze that had found its way through the side door to ruffle his hair.

"Take it now." The Old Man took his hand and placed it where his had been on the wheel. "I'll be with you this time, and there'll be no more accidents. So let's begin by not ramming the Swan Hill wharf, if you please."

Patrick was afraid to look away, afraid to think of what the barge behind him was doing.

"I'm going to hit the wharf," he worried. "And what about that other paddle steamer there?"

He pointed at the other boat. It was not the *Gem*.

"You're not going to hit anything." The Old Man's voice was calmer, but Patrick noticed his eyes were shut.

Maybe he can do this in his sleep, thought Patrick, *but it's a sure thing I can't*.

Still, they coasted in to the Swan Hill wharf softly, with the Old Man shouting instructions over the railing. He seemed to have no trouble getting his message across. Even Wesley and Hamilton stood on the deck, wrapped in blankets, watching the show.

"Right full rudder, Patrick!" hollered the Old Man, twirling his right hand in the air. "Clockwise, understand?"

"Patrick?" Mrs. McWaid looked up at him curiously. "What are you doing?"

"It's all right, Sarah," the Old Man assured her. "They need to earn their keep."

Feeling his mother's eyes on him, Patrick nodded and twirled the wheel after thinking for only a moment: *Which direction does a clock's hand travel?* With the paddles on each side slowly turning backward, he saw the lights on the wharf next to them slowly back up, as the back end of the *Lady Elisabeth* found its way to the shore. It would be a tight fit; the wharf was much smaller than the one at Echuca and much older looking. Luke and Jefferson had gripped their barge tightly to the outside corner of the paddle steamer, and now they both watched carefully.

"Perfect!" cried Luke. "Good job!"

His friend was a little early in his praise; they slammed into the wharf with a bump that sent a shiver through the boat. Still, they had made it. Patrick took a deep breath and sighed as a couple of men on the wharf helped them tie up.

It could have been a lot worse, he thought, and the Old Man told him the same thing as the steam engine and the paddle wheels fell silent. Patrick's mother ducked back inside the salon without another word.

"Say, mate." Hamilton stopped in his tracks and licked his finger as he noted the koala perched on Michael's shoulder. "Wherever did you get one of those creatures?"

Michael looked like he wasn't sure if he should say anything. He glanced around for help, but everyone else was gone. Unseen and quiet, Patrick looked down at what was happening from the deck above.

"Someone gave him to me," replied Michael in a little voice. He tried to back away, but their guest blocked his way.

"Does he bite?" wondered Hamilton. He put out a finger to stroke the cat-sized animal's soft brown fur, and Christopher let him touch his ear.

Michael shook his head. "He's nice. Sleeps, mostly. Doesn't bite." Christopher cooperated by showing them a big koala yawn.

"I've never actually seen one of these creatures up close," remarked the man.

"That's what everybody says."

"Hmm." Hamilton must have had an idea, and he went on as if he was talking to himself. "A tame koala bear has to be worth a gold mine for a pretty English woman in Sydney. Just think, if we could sell it there . . . Or maybe even a koala skin hat?"

Michael tried to back away but didn't get very far.

"What do you want for him?" The man reached into his pocket for a coin and held it out in front of him. "I was only joking about the koala-skin hat. Nobody's going to hurt the little fellow. Here's sixpence. You'd like that, wouldn't you. Sixpence for the little beast?"

By this time Michael was backed up against the boat, and Patrick tried to think of what he could drop on the man's head.

Sixpence! Patrick gritted his teeth. *He thinks he can trick a little boy with sixpence—hardly enough to buy candy!*

The man laughed. "Well, now, I was just kidding about the sixpence, boy. You're smarter than that, aren't you? So here's a pound. That sounds much better, doesn't it?"

Michael hesitated for just a moment. "Would that be enough to help my grandpa buy back his boat?"

Patrick couldn't believe his ears, but then he remembered what their father had told Michael just a few days ago. *"We're all doing what we can to help your grandfather. . . ."*

"No—" Hamilton began, but then he stopped short and fingered the coin in front of him. "I mean, no doubt it would, my young friend. That much money would be a very big help to your grandpa. Perhaps you might also have enough left over to purchase him a pair of spectacles."

Michael looked at his pet, and even from where he stood, Patrick was sure there were tears in his brother's eyes. Michael whispered something in the animal's ear.

He can't do that! thought Patrick.

"The koala isn't for sale," Patrick called down. Hamilton nearly jumped out of his shoes and stared up at Patrick.

"I say, there!" scolded the man. "Didn't your mother ever tell you it's not polite to scare people like that?"

Patrick crossed his arms and didn't move. He had seen enough of Mr. Hamilton.

"It's Michael's koala, and he would never sell it."

Mr. Hamilton wasn't giving up, though, not just yet.

"Well, why don't we let the little lad speak for himself? Sounds as if he wants to help his grandfather. And a pound is a lot of money."

The man looked back again, but Patrick had given his brother just enough time to step away. Hamilton reached out, but he wasn't quick enough.

"Run, Michael!" yelled Patrick.

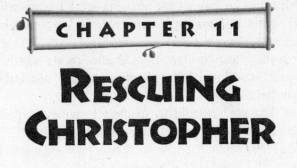

CHAPTER 11

RESCUING CHRISTOPHER

"You'll regret it, boy!" Hamilton called after Michael. "No one else is going to give you that much money for a koala. I'm a generous man, but I'm not overly patient."

Patrick backed away from the upper railing and frowned. He heard the door to the side of the salon slam as Mr. Hamilton returned inside.

Was that a threat? wondered Patrick.

Threat or no, Mr. Hamilton and his big friend remained on board for the rest of the night—mostly to eat, but then they invited themselves to spend the evening on board. Hamilton sat across the big oak salon table from the Old Man, finishing off another piece of bread topped with cheese.

"After all," Hamilton was saying, "it's the least you can do, after running us down in the river." He leaned forward and motioned toward Wesley, who was studying his food. "And we don't want Wesley getting angry again."

I hope they're not spending the night, thought Patrick.

"Could you give us a hand, Patrick?" His father staggered under the weight of a big wooden carton marked with a downriver address. "There are a whole lot more where this one came from."

"How about that?" smiled Jefferson. He gripped the other side of the crate. "A little extra cargo, a few extra dollars—I mean, shillings. Maybe we'll be able to buy back the other half of the boat after all with the money we get out of this."

"Don't get your hopes up," warned Mr. McWaid. He grunted as they strained to lower the boxes to a level spot on deck. One of them had the words "Farm Equipment" stenciled on its side.

"Easy . . ." said Luke. He didn't look as muscled as Jeff, but he more than held his own.

By the time the boys finished loading the boxes, pumping more water, and checking the barges, the lantern was already out in the *Lady Elisabeth*'s salon. Patrick wasn't sure how late it was, but suddenly he could hardly keep his eyes open.

"You've been working hard." His father clapped him on the back. "Get some rest, and we'll be off again at daybreak. Your grandpa is anxious to get going again."

"Only twenty-two more days," said Jefferson, poking his head in at the door behind them. Patrick didn't need the reminder. He stumbled over to his bedroll in the dark corner and was nearly asleep before his head hit the pillow.

"You did *what*?" Patrick's grandpa didn't seem to mind that it was barely light. Of course, there was no chance for Patrick to sleep through anything else.

"I thought it would help," Michael's voice warbled on the edge of bawling. When Patrick opened his eyes, his brother had begun in earnest. Their mother put her arm around her youngest son.

"Oh, Michael."

He buried his face in Mrs. McWaid's shoulder, and the tears came in waves.

"What's going on?" Patrick asked, but he had a sinking feeling in the pit of his stomach. "Where's your koala, Michael?"

"He gave me five pounds for Christopher," sniffled Michael. "I didn't really want to sell him, but I thought it would help Grandpa. I thought it was a lot of money."

"Surely you know the worth of a paddle steamer better than

that. . . ." began the Old Man. "Five pounds is half a month's wages, but . . ."

He stood awkwardly in the middle of the salon. Mrs. McWaid shot him a quick warning with her eyes.

"It doesn't matter what he knew," said their mother. "He was just trying to help you any way he could. It was a fine thing he did."

"You mean Mr. Hamilton?" asked Becky. "You sold the koala to Mr. Hamilton?"

By that time Michael could hardly speak, he was sobbing so hard. He nodded sadly as he sobbed.

"I . . . I thought . . ." That was all Patrick needed to hear. He sprang up from his bedroll.

"Where is he? I told him yesterday that the koala wasn't for sale. I'm going to—"

"You're not going anywhere," interrupted the Old Man, holding him back by the shoulder.

"Yes, I am," Patrick shot back. He felt the temperature rising in his cheeks at the thought of Mr. Hamilton taking advantage of Michael. If only he had been there . . .

"Ah, young Michael." The Old Man's voice had softened. "You meant well, didn't you?"

Michael began to wail all over again; the Old Man tried to quiet him by patting Michael's head with his rough hand.

"I'm afraid we're going to need a whole lot more than five pounds to save the *Lady E.*"

Michael dug into his pocket and held out the money as his grandpa continued.

"I'll see what I can do in town. You shouldn't be selling your pet for your old grandpa."

The Old Man squinted at Michael, took the money, and turned to go.

"I'll go with you," Patrick volunteered.

"No," answered the Old Man, and the firmness of the captain's voice had returned. "It's my business, and mine alone. I'll fetch the animal if he's to be found."

Patrick looked back on the deck, but of course the fishermen's rowboat was gone.

"They're miles upriver by now," said Luke.

"Oh, and, Johnny." The Old Man paused as he stepped off the boat. "See that you have steam up by the time I get back. We've wasted too much time here already."

For the next hour they scurried about, straightening up the paddle steamer and getting ready to leave as soon as the Old Man returned. Smoke billowing out of their stacks told Patrick they would soon have enough steam to turn the paddle wheel; he listened for the telltale hissing sound. Luke stood on top of the wool barge, hands on his hips, looking up the river.

"I can't believe he would take advantage of a little boy like that," he said to no one in particular. "But with that fellow's appetite, I wouldn't be surprised if he . . ."

Luke didn't finish, and Patrick was glad that Michael hadn't heard him. Michael was still sniffling, but he was done crying, and he tried to look brave as he stood at the edge of the afterdeck with Patrick.

"Do you think Grandpa will get Christopher back, Patrick?"

Patrick winced at the thought of the cuddly little bear hauled into a smoky pub, maybe tossed around like a toy, then auctioned off to the highest bidder. Michael hadn't been the only one who was attached to the little animal.

"I hope so, Michael."

By that time his father had worked up a full head of steam in the *Lady E*, and everyone stood ready to go. Everyone except Jefferson.

"What happened to Jeff?" Patrick asked his sister. He had gotten used to the fact that in most cases she usually knew exactly where the older boy was. But Becky only shook her head.

"I think he ran up to see if he could help," explained their father, coming out of the engine room for a breath of air.

"Speaking of Jeff." Luke pointed to the town of Swan Hill from his lookout. Jefferson was headed their way at a fast trot. He vaulted over a couple of barrels, clicked his heels, and landed right on the middle of the wool barge.

"Well?" asked Patrick.

"Did you see him?" asked Becky.

Jefferson got to his feet and nodded as he caught his breath. He was grinning from ear to ear.

"You should have seen your grandpa in action," he told them. "I've never seen him so . . . well, he was in command, that's for sure. Just marched right up to a couple of old pubs, pounded on the doors, and dragged a few sleepy innkeepers out of bed."

"Really?" Michael followed the story with wide, excited eyes. "And then what?"

Mr. McWaid chuckled and looked up at the wharf. "Maybe he'll tell you himself."

As their grandpa stepped onto the Swan Hill wharf, they could see him holding a little wiggling burlap sack. He held it out in front of him as if he didn't want to touch it.

"Let go the lines!" he barked. "Johnny, where's my steam?"

Their father let loose with a short toot of the steam whistle.

"Don't waste our steam on noise!" the Old Man scolded him. With a quick glance over his shoulder at the town, he climbed back aboard the paddle-wheeler with his sack.

"You got him!" shouted Michael, running up to his grandpa with a big hug.

"That's a fact." He set the sack down gently on the deck, and Michael excitedly undid the string at the top. "And now I'll thank you to keep him away from me. He's an expensive little bear."

"Did you have to buy him back, Grandpa?" Becky wanted to know, but he obviously wasn't in the story-telling mood. Without an answer he climbed up to his perch in the steering house. Patrick followed.

"It took four innkeepers," Jefferson explained to the others, "but he finally found him. Owner of the hardware store bought him last night for practically nothing. But your grandpa had to pay just about everything we made from this new cargo just to get him back."

Patrick tried to concentrate on his new job, getting the *Lady Elisabeth* out of her spot between two other paddle steamers without scratching the sides.

"And you know what else, Patrick?" Jefferson pointed at his friend.

"Can you tell me later, Jeff? I'm—"

Jefferson went on with his story. "Warburton. Remember him?"

Now even the Old Man was paying attention.

"Of course we remember Warburton." Patrick tried to reckon with his eyes how much room they had to spare in front of them.

"Well, sounds like he left town just before we arrived."

"So we just missed him?"

"That's what I heard. And it's the same story all over again. The fellow spends a lot of money in a big hurry, and then he leaves on the next paddle steamer out of town. We're not sure which one, though."

Patrick sighed. "All that money down the drain."

"Mind the barge, now," the Old Man reminded as their paddle wheels began to turn. "And you, Jefferson, you'd best be getting along."

"Yessir." Jefferson saluted as he always did and bounded down the ladder. A moment later he stationed himself on the narrow deck of the barge, just below where Luke was steering.

"All right, Johnny," shouted the captain of the *Lady Elisabeth*. "Give us full steam."

The *Lady E* slowly slipped away from her berth.

"Hold it there, please!" shouted a man from the wharf, running up to the paddle steamer. If it were Jefferson, he would have made it easily across the water. But Patrick saw a look of panic on the man's face as he realized that the paddle steamer was farther away from the wharf than he had hoped. It was too late, though, and the stranger teetered on the edge of the wharf, about to fall.

CHAPTER 12

NEW PASSENGER

"What kind of foolishness?" wondered the Old Man, but there was nothing they could do but watch the man take a dive into the river. The man grabbed wildly at the air, made a few windmills with his arms, and finally found a grip on one of the pilings.

"Hold it there!" shouted the Old Man, and he spun the wheel back. It would not be easy to back the *Lady Elisabeth* to the wharf alone; next to impossible to return with the big wool barge.

"What are we doing?" yelled Jefferson.

"Hold on!" the Old Man yelled back, and he turned his gaze to the lower deck. "Reverse, Johnny, do you hear me?"

"I hear you," echoed Mr. McWaid from inside the engine room. "Reverse."

Even though they weren't going very fast to begin with, the paddle wheels churned up a spray of water as they slowly came to a stop. The barge thumped them and almost sent Patrick flying, until they once again stopped and reversed back toward the wharf.

In the meantime the stranger on the wharf had crawled back up to safety.

"I think it's a priest," Patrick whispered to his grandpa, but he didn't need to explain. It was pretty obvious, after all, by the man's stiff white collar under a black coat and black pants. The priest was young looking, maybe in his twenties, and his large frame poked way too far out of the ends of his sleeves. On top of that, he looked as if he needed a shave.

"Throw him a line, Becky." The Old Man sighed as if giving in to a pesky child. Becky didn't hear and looked back over her shoulder with a question on her face.

"I said, throw him a line." Their grandpa crossed his arms and stood stiffly on the deck next to his wheelhouse. "Johnny, hold off on that steam."

The young priest smiled as he caught the rope that was thrown his way, and he expertly looped the line over a piling to pull the paddle steamer back in a few feet. When he leaned back, his arms seemed to nearly burst the sleeves of his shirt.

"Awfully good of you to wait for me, mates." He smiled, showing a full set of gleaming white teeth. "I'm Father Christie, and I'm looking for a ride downriver to Murray Bridge."

"We're no passenger vessel, Father," announced the Old Man, squinting at the deck below. "With no real accommodations such as you might be expecting."

"Ah, but I'll not be expecting much," replied the man. Without waiting for an answer, he unlooped the rope with a flip of his wrist, stepped across, and looked up at the Old Man. "And I can certainly pay my own way."

Patrick tried not to stare from his station at the wheel of the *Lady Elisabeth*. The Old Man didn't answer right away, so the man in black pulled a money bag from his jacket pocket and produced a fistful of coins. "Will ten pounds be adequate for the trip down?"

The man must have noticed how the Old Man's jaw dropped to the deck, and he quickly pulled out several more large coins. "No use quibbling. The parish has been exceedingly generous with me. Shall we make it fifteen?"

Fifteen pounds? Patrick tried not to gawk at all the money the man offered. More than most rivermen made in a month, he knew, and maybe more than enough to make the trip up and down the river several times.

"I *do* wonder, however, if we might leave promptly?" The priest looked over his shoulder at the town, but the early morning street was deserted.

"We can make room," said Mr. McWaid, coming up out of the engine room to see what was happening.

"God bless you," he said as he pressed the coins into Mr. McWaid's gritty palm and quickly disappeared inside.

"All right, then, we seem to have a passenger." The Old Man returned to the river while Mr. McWaid stood frozen on the deck, staring at the fistful of coins. "Johnny, are we still ready?"

"Aye, Captain." Patrick's father finally stuffed the money into his pocket and hurried inside to tend his engine.

With paddle wheels churning once again, Patrick eased the *Lady Elisabeth* into the main current of the Murray and they slipped away from Swan Hill. The Old Man gently guided him with his hand and with quiet comments like "a little left, there," or "watch for the shallow spot up ahead."

He's steering me from memory, thought Patrick.

Patrick did his best to follow, knowing that it was only his eyes that kept them from running aground, or worse. He was concentrating so hard that he almost missed a commotion to the side and a bit behind them, back on shore. Two men on horses had come galloping up to the Swan Hill wharf, their shouts fading in the distance.

"What's he like, Becky?" Patrick asked at lunchtime when his sister came to relieve him at the wheel. "Is he really a Catholic priest? *Father* Christie?"

Becky shook her head. "Says he's a Methodist circuit preacher. Calls himself the Right Reverend Mr. Charles Christie, but . . ." Her voice trailed off, and she didn't finish her sentence.

"But what?" Patrick handed over the wheel to his sister and allowed himself to relax. "You look like you're trying to solve a mystery."

Becky checked the chart, then looked back up as the Old Man pointed out the next bend.

"It's no mystery. He seems a nice enough man. Just different."

"Different, sure," mumbled the Old Man. "If I'd have known there was so much money in preaching, I might have listened a little harder for the call."

"Grandpa!" Becky scolded him gently. "Don't you think he was just trying to be fair?"

"Foolish is a better word for it. I might have transported his entire flock for what he paid me."

"What I don't understand is why he was in such a hurry," said Patrick.

Becky shook her head, but it was her turn to concentrate. Patrick decided to head back downstairs to see this Right Reverend Mr. Charles Christie for himself.

"Ah, but I'm just a simple country pastor." The Reverend Christie's voice drifted up from downstairs in between the constant musical slap of the paddle wheels. He stood up and smiled when he saw Patrick come into the salon.

"And you must be Master Patrick. I've already heard so much about you."

Patrick raised his eyebrows. "You have?"

"All good things, of course." Their passenger put out his hand. "I'm the Right Reverend Mr. Charles Christie."

Patrick's eyed bulged at the viselike grip of the rough hand, and he thought he heard the bones in his hand pop.

"Didn't you say your name was *Father* Christie?" Michael wanted to know. The man laughed.

"No, no. Did I say that?" The reverend smiled again.

"When you were running to stop us." Michael set his jaw. "I heard you."

Come to think of it, remembered Patrick, *I'm pretty sure that's what he said, too.*

"Ah, well, perhaps a slip of the tongue." Reverend Christie pushed out his chair and leaned back with his hands knit behind his head. "I find that people are a bit more comfortable with me if I tell them my name is Father Christie—particularly Irish folk like yourselves. Denominations are such foolishness, don't you think?"

Patrick looked at his mother. She obviously hadn't told him that they were Presbyterians.

"Well, in any case," continued the Reverend, "I'm very glad to have made a connection with such a fine vessel. We seem to be proceeding at full speed."

"Where did you attend seminary, Reverend Christie?" Mrs. McWaid asked as she fixed a pot of tea.

"Uh, well, now . . ." The reverend checked the shoreline before he answered. "Are you familiar with London?"

"No, sir, I hadn't been out of Ireland until recently."

A smile played on the edge of Reverend Christie's lips. "Good, well, I attended theological school, that is, seminary, back in London."

"I see." Mrs. McWaid placed cups of steaming tea on the salon table. Michael studied him closely.

"You don't look like a reverend to me," announced Michael, never taking his eyes off their guest. Reverend Christie nearly spit out his tea.

"Goodness, Reverend, is it too hot?" Mrs. McWaid picked up a napkin to help, but he held up his hand.

"No, no, child. I'm fine, really. Just clumsy. First I nearly fall off the old wharf. Now I choke on a cup of tea." The reverend searched the shoreline as he spoke.

Patrick looked out to see what Reverend Christie might be searching for, but all he could see was the tangled shoreline of eucalyptus shrub and the distant flatlands. They were nearing the part of the river the Old Man had called the Mallee, and they were still making good time, even with the barge.

The barge! Sometimes Patrick almost forgot Jefferson and Luke were back there, and he could barely see them standing watch over their mountain of wool bales.

As they wound through the Mallee, the Reverend Christie told them stories about the bush, about preaching stations he had traveled to, dry outposts with few white people—only aborigines, kangaroos, emus, and wallabies. Michael held on to every word.

"Ayers Rock—the natives call it Uluru," said the reverend, lifting up his arms to describe the desert landmark, the towering rock in the middle of the Australian outback. "They say it's magical."

"Magical?" Michael wasn't so sure. Reverend Christie smiled, showing his big yellow teeth.

"You'll have to see for yourself sometime, lad. Maybe someday when you don't have school lessons every day, you could go on an expedition there."

Mrs. McWaid didn't object, so Patrick guessed she was trying to be polite to their guest. The teacups rattled and they looked down at the table in surprise.

"What now?" asked the reverend as his teacup scooted off the edge of the table into his lap.

Patrick grabbed at the flying teapot, but he missed and nearly fell face first into the table. The floor beneath him seemed to roll.

"I think we hit a sandbar!" shouted Patrick. But he knew it couldn't be so. He looked out the back window just in time to see the bottom of their barge turn upside down, like a turtle flipping over in the water. Upstairs, the Old man shouted down at them.

"Stop the engine, Johnny! The barge is turning over!"

For a moment Patrick thought the barge would pull them under, too. When they ran out on the trembling deck, it was obvious the barge seemed to have a mind of its own as it thrashed like a living thing, a wild animal on the end of its leash. They stared helplessly, alone in the middle of a narrow bend in the river, as water streamed off its mossy underside. No other paddle steamers were in sight.

"Jefferson!" called Becky. She half slid, half fell down the ladder, none too gracefully.

"Jefferson! Luke!" Patrick and the others joined in the shout, all except the bewildered Reverend Christie, who stood in the door-way with his hands knit together either in terror or prayer or both. In a moment Mr. McWaid joined them, but he could only stand and stare.

CHAPTER 13

WOOL RESCUE

Patrick started to take off his shoes, but he couldn't see anyone to rescue. The barge just continued to roll and churn up the muddy river bottom they had dragged across.

"I knew that barge was top-heavy," said the Old Man. "I never should have agreed to haul it."

"It's not your fault," Mr. McWaid tried to tell his father, but the Old Man just stood at the edge of the deck, unsure of where to swing his rope.

"I've been around that bend a hundred times before," continued the Old Man, staring at the water and shaking his head. "But this time the barge must have caught on the bottom, and it just plain rolled."

"It wasn't your fault," said Mr. McWaid.

"I should have known."

Mr. McWaid shook his head.

"Jefferson!" Becky cried once more. "He doesn't swim so well."

He doesn't swim at all, thought Patrick.

By that time the paddle wheels had stopped turning, but the barge was still shuddering and quivering as if it were struggling for breath. One by one the bales of wool broke free and came bubbling to the surface. Patrick stood with his head in his hands, not believing what he knew he was seeing. It had all happened much too fast.

"Jeff?" he whispered. "Luke?"

Patrick could only imagine what had become of his two friends, riding the top of the overloaded barge. Had Luke been at the wheel, or Jefferson? As best he could tell, both of them were now trapped under the massive load. Another bale popped up and drifted past them, then another. Still they stared. A minute went by.

How long can they hold their breath under there? As more bales of wool popped to the surface, though, he heard another sound. Becky looked at him.

"I heard it, too!" she said.

Gasping. Someone gasping for air. Patrick listened again, and then he was sure of it.

"Over here!" yelled a small voice from behind the overturned barge, just as several more wool bales bobbed free and the entire load started to right itself. As the barge slowly bobbed back to upright, they saw two heads in the water, then Luke waving an arm weakly.

"There!" Patrick pointed, and the Old Man threw his line at the survivors. A minute later they were back on deck, dripping and sputtering.

"We thought you were gone." Becky brought them a rough towel to dry off. "When we didn't hear anything . . ."

"Aw, we were fine," replied Jefferson, rubbing his dark hair dry. "We just had to hold our breath awhile before that big monster tipped back up. Fact, we were catching our breath for a minute there, trying to figure out a way to swim around."

"He was holding on to my belt the whole time," gasped Luke.

"And you were trying to pull my hair out!" answered Jefferson. Everyone had to laugh.

The Old Man shook his head. "Soon as it dumped its load, the barge righted itself. Just like a duck, it was."

"And while we're standing here chatting," said Jefferson, "all the rest of the wool is floating downstream."

He picked a pole off the deck and reached out to snag a passing bale.

"Just like that?" asked Becky. "You two nearly drown, and now you just want us to rescue the wool as if nothing happened?"

"Nothing *did* happen," insisted Jefferson.

"Right," agreed Luke. "We're alive and well. And all we have to do now is load the bales that fell off back on deck. At least the barge isn't so top-heavy anymore."

"Maybe so." The Old Man frowned. "But I'd just as soon you didn't give your lives provin' the fact."

Jefferson swatted the comment back with his hand and lassoed a rope around the closest wool bale.

"No harm done. I wasn't going to let Luke get away with my hair."

Patrick could tell the older boy was trying his best to act as if nothing much had happened. But Jefferson's hands were shaking.

"Here, now," insisted Mrs. McWaid. "You two boys can at least step inside to dry up."

Luke and Jefferson both shook their heads.

"Thank you, no, ma'am," said Luke. "Right now we'd better round up this wool."

Which is what they did, drifting down the Murray River barely faster than the current, yet fast enough to catch up with the runaway bales of wool. Each one was far too heavy for one person to lift.

"I see another one!" yelled Michael. He had already spotted four.

The Old Man kept a protective eye out behind and ahead. While Patrick steered, Becky kept an eye on the barge, just in case.

"I'm sure it's safe now," said the Old Man, but Becky hardly blinked. Jefferson, on the other hand, waved and smiled from his perch back on the barge. The top of the load was at least ten feet lower since they had dumped nearly half the wool. Patrick wasn't sure how the rest of the bales had stayed tied to the barge, but there they were.

"Can't spend all day on this," mumbled the Old Man, checking his pocket watch. Patrick knew what he meant, but still they snagged bale after bale. Most were barely afloat and dripped water like wet dogs when they finally managed to wrestle them on deck.

"That's all but two," said Mrs. McWaid. She marked another notch in a small notebook with a sliver of charcoal-tipped wood. Michael and Patrick helped the Reverend Christie with the loading, leaning back on the rope when he did.

"That's the strongest pastor I've ever met up with," whispered Mr. McWaid as they slid another bale on the side deck to drip-dry.

"Good eating and plenty of prayer!" quipped the reverend as he easily shoved a bale into a clear spot on the deck. He also seemed to have good hearing.

"Well, Reverend," said Mrs. McWaid, poking her head out the side window. "We'll look forward to a proper worship service here on board Sunday morning."

The reverend stopped for a moment, then smiled and straightened out. "Ah yes, of course. A worship service."

Sunday morning dawned bright and clear on the river, a perfect spring day. As usual, Patrick kept up his search for the *Gem*, hoping to sight the paddle steamer Warburton might still be riding. And as usual, he saw nothing.

They had tied up for only a few hours the night before to stock up on firewood for the steam engine, and Patrick hadn't even heard when his father and grandpa and the Reverend Christie slipped out of their beds to work on the loading. The few days he traveled with them, Christie had been surprisingly willing to help out with the work—helping to load wood and keep the boiler going. Still, Patrick didn't like having an extra person on board. He frowned when he thought of their passenger.

The steam engine was sputtering and hissing, almost ready to go. "Stand by to make way!" shouted the captain from his high perch. Mrs. McWaid pulled a knitted blanket over her shoulders, crossed her arms, and marched to the deck.

"The Reverend Christie has kindly consented to lead us in a

worship service," she called up in her sweetest tone, "if you'd care to come down and join us. This *is* the Lord's day, after all."

The Old Man sighed and checked his pocket watch. Patrick knew that he wasn't one of the paddle-steamer captains who stopped his boat on Sunday, though there weren't very many who actually did.

"Thirty minutes, then," the Old Man shouted back. "Though we should have been under way hours ago. We've got only eighteen days to get to Goolwa."

"Thank you," Mrs. McWaid smiled. "But how about yourself?"

The Old Man ignored the invitation. "We're headed down the river in thirty minutes, worship service or no worship service."

Mrs. McWaid looked to her husband, who only shrugged.

"I'm sorry, dear," he told her quietly. "I can't change him."

"Well, then, shall we start?" The Reverend Christie stood at the front of the salon while everyone else found a seat either around the table or on the floor. The congregation numbered eight, counting the koala. Mr. McWaid checked the deck once more, then shook his head.

"He's not coming. Let's go ahead."

Reverend Christie rocked up on his heels and held out his hands.

"The Lord be with you," he intoned, as if he was expecting them to answer. Patrick looked at his sister out of the corner of his eye.

"And also with you." Mrs. McWaid was the only one to answer.

"Why don't you have a Bible?" asked Michael, who sat closest to the pastor.

"A Bible?" wondered Reverend Christie. "I . . . uh . . ."

"Here." Becky held out a worn, dog-eared volume that looked as if it had come through a hurricane. "You can borrow mine."

Their pastor smiled. "Thank you, child. I gave mine to a poor parishioner in the last town. He had no Bible and no shoes, poor soul."

"What are you going to preach about?" Michael asked, too quickly for Becky to quiet him with her hand. The reverend leafed through the Bible before he answered.

"From the book of . . . er, Abraham," he answered. "Does anyone else have a Bible?"

Mr. McWaid lifted his, a larger one than even Becky's. The Reverend Christie's face fell just a bit, but he quickly recovered.

"I see. Well, there's no need to follow along. I'll tell you everything you need to know."

They stared at the reverend, who shifted nervously from foot to foot and rubbed his chin. Even Christopher stopped eating long enough to gaze at the man with his big, dark eyes. Patrick noticed the man still had not shaved since joining them on the *Lady Elisabeth*.

"Eh, but first, shall we sing a hymn?" continued the Reverend Christie.

"Which one?" asked Becky.

He lobbed the question right back. "You tell me your favorite."

" 'The Solid Rock,' " suggested Michael. "We sang that on the ship with Ma, on the way to Australia when the waves got high. Do you remember that, Patrick?"

Patrick smiled and nodded. "I remember. That was just before Jeff fell into the water."

"Not that story again," groaned Jefferson. "Please don't tell that story."

"Well, then." The reverend raised his hand like a choir director. "Let's sing 'The Solid Rock.' I mean, let us begin. One, two . . ."

Somehow they got started, with Becky's clear, true voice leading the way and their father's steady baritone balancing the family choir. Even Luke and Jefferson joined in, stumbling over some of the words but managing to add a lot of noise. But though their song leader waved his hand up and down and moved his lips, Patrick couldn't make out his voice.

" 'When darkness veils his lovely face,' " sang Patrick, " 'I rest on his unchanging grace . . .' "

"Don't you know the song?" Michael asked Reverend Christie after they had finished the second verse.

Reverend Christie cleared his throat and buried his nose in the

Bible he held, ignoring Michael's question. They finished the fourth verse.

"Well?" persisted Michael. "Don't you?"

"Michael." Becky hushed her little brother, but the reverend put up his hand and smiled to tell her it was all right.

"No worries, child." He took a deep breath. "But I must confess I am not a grand singer. Chances are you would prefer not hearing my attempts at song."

"Michael, you're being rude." Becky scolded him again. Michael looked back at her as if he didn't understand a word.

"Let's have another hymn," put in the reverend.

Michael suggested "Be Thou My Vision," an Irish hymn.

"You know the words?" asked Reverend Christie, but Michael only smiled and sang a little more loudly the part about "Riches I heed not, nor man's empty praise," and then through the last verse:

High King of heaven, my victory won,
May I reach heaven's joys, O bright heav'n's Sun!
Heart of my own heart, whatever befall,
Still be my vision, O Ruler of all.

They all caught their breath at the end and waited for Reverend Christie to begin his talk. He cleared his throat seriously, then opened the Bible and peered up over the edge at Michael.

"So, young man, do you know the words to the Bible, too?"

"Some of them. My ma used to make me memorize verses when we lived back in Ireland."

"So you know the book of Abraham?"

Michael shook his head and wrinkled his forehead.

"Ah well," replied Reverend Christie. "Now, Abraham, he was the one who said, 'The Lord helps them that help themselves,' was he not?"

"There is no book of Abraham," announced Patrick. "And that saying isn't in the Bible."

The preacher smiled and pointed at him. "Right you are. You have just passed my first test. I wanted to see if you were listening."

We're listening, thought Patrick. *I'm just not sure what we're hearing.*

"Bright boy you have here, Mr. and Mrs. McWaid." He smiled again and pulled at his collar as if it had suddenly heated up. "Very bright boy. I'll tell you what, though, Patrick. I know this is isn't a church, and we're . . . you know, quite informal here. But how about if I finish the sermon without any more interruptions, eh?"

"Sorry." Patrick nodded.

"Well, then, as I was saying, the topic for my sermon is, ah . . ." He leafed from page to page of the Bible, squinting at the fine print. Finally he closed his eyes, leafed through the pages, and with a smile planted his finger at random.

"Here it is, from above," he declared. "One of my very favorite portions."

Patrick leaned over to see where the magic finger had come down, but the reverend pulled back the Bible protectively and cleared his throat.

"Would you like me to bring you a glass of water, Reverend?" asked Mrs. McWaid.

The reverend nodded quickly. "Yes, that would be very nice. He looked down again at the page where his finger had stopped, and his smile froze before he cleared his throat.

"I think what I'll do is begin reading here in the book of . . . Numbers, yes, the twenty-sixth chapter." He strained to look closer at the page, then held it out in front of him. Finally he held it out to Michael. "Pardon me, child, but I must have left my spectacles back at the mission. Would you kindly read that name for me?"

"Issachar," read Michael.

"IS-a-car," the reverend repeated the Bible name carefully, then he lowered his eyes again to read. "Hmm, yes. Very good. Now, it says here, 'Of the sons of Issachar after their families: of Tola, the family of the Tolaites, of . . . Pua, the family of the . . .'"

"Punites." Michael was reading over his shoulder, and the reverend smiled back at him.

"Punites, correct. 'Of Jashub, the family of the Jashubites: of Shimron, the family of the Shimronites . . . according to those that were numbered of them, threescore and four thousand and three hundred.' "

The man skipped down the page with his finger, and his jaw dropped.

"There are a lot more names in this chapter," began Michael. "Aren't you going to keep reading them?"

"Yes, well, as I said, this is a very special chapter for me, but I think I've read the best part already."

The others waited silently. Patrick's parents looked politely mystified.

Where is this going? wondered Patrick.

The reverend went on. "All that means two things, dear friends. Ah . . . well, it means that families in those days were rather large, and they gave their children rather odd-sounding names. Now, I know of several large families with many oddly named children. . . ."

The reverend somehow managed to fill up the next ten minutes with his unusual stories, most of which didn't make a lot of sense, except that they were about large families. The reverend pounded his Bible as he spoke and ended suddenly with a loud "Amen!" when he seemed to have run out of stories—or breath.

"Um, amen?" Mr. McWaid looked at his wife with a raised eyebrow, but she just smiled and gritted her teeth. Patrick had seen that look before when an older woman from their church in Dublin had arrived at their door and presented them with a horrible-looking Christmas cake made from what Michael thought had to be fish heads. Their mother had held them back with a firm grip and they had smiled and said thank-you just the same.

"That was very, ah . . ." Mrs. McWaid paused after the service was over, and Patrick waited to see how his mother would choose her words. "Very unique. I'd never heard the Bible described quite the way you did."

Reverend Christie's face brightened. "You liked it, then?"

Mrs. McWaid smiled and repeated herself. "Very unique."

"Unique isn't the word for it," Patrick whispered to his sister as they climbed the ladder to the wheelhouse. The Old Man was pacing the upper deck with his arms crossed. "More like odd, if you ask me. Have you ever seen a pastor like him?"

Becky shook her head.

"A pastor who thinks 'Abraham' is a book in the Bible?" Patrick went on. "You want to know what I think?"

"I'm not sure," answered his sister, taking the wheel. "But it sounds as if you're going to tell me."

"That's right. I think he's a fraud. I don't think he's who he says he is."

"Do tell?" The Old Man raised his eyebrows as they slowly gathered steam and pulled out into the river. The *Lady Elisabeth* parted what morning mist the sun hadn't already burned away, and even over the sound of the paddles they could hear the wail of a wood duck as it took off downstream.

"That's right." Patrick stomped his foot and hit his fist in the palm of his hand. "And you know what else?"

"Patrick," began Becky. She didn't look at him; she was concentrating on the way ahead. "I don't think you'd better do anything rash."

"Rash?" This time Patrick could feel the color of his cheeks. "I'm just saying somebody needs to find out who this 'Reverend' really is. I'm going to go down there right now and . . ."

Patrick didn't need to say anything else because the reverend shouted a hello from the foot of the ladder.

"Well, now." Their grandpa wiped the grin from his face. "Perhaps you'll have a chance to test your idea."

Sure enough, the Reverend Christie was on his way up.

"I'll say one thing for the fellow," whispered the Old Man. "His timing is perfect."

CHAPTER 14

CONFESSION

Patrick took a deep breath as Reverend Christie entered the crowded wheelhouse. Becky kept one hand on the steering wheel, the other on Patrick's elbow.

"Don't—" she whispered, but Patrick wouldn't listen. He crossed his arms and poked his chin at the man.

The book of Abraham, he says! Patrick told himself once more. *This is no preacher.*

"So this is where you navigate the boat," said the reverend, smiling as he stepped up to examine the brass compass that hung on swivels between the steering wheel and the front window. Patrick pointed at the man's face.

"You're not a pastor!" The words spilled out of Patrick's mouth.

At first the reverend looked amused, and he smiled even more widely. "I'm not? What, pray, is this starched white collar for, then?"

Becky squeezed Patrick's elbow more tightly. He pulled it away.

"You may look like a reverend, but you don't know anything about the Bible. I don't know who you really are, but I don't believe anything you say."

This time the Reverend Christie looked as if he had been hit in the face. His eyes filled with tears, and he turned away.

"Heaven forgive me for what I've done," he whispered.

"What did you say?" Patrick demanded as the reverend turned back to face his accuser.

"I said, I pray you'll find it in your heart to forgive me for what I've done. But first you must hear me out."

I was right! Patrick crossed his arms and waited for the impostor to explain.

"You see, I've only meant it for good," said the man. He took a handkerchief out of his hip pocket and wiped his eyes, then blew his nose. "And yes, it's true, I'm truly not a reverend, as I represented myself."

Patrick looked at his sister as if to say, "I told you so," as the man continued his story.

"After my father was shot by bushrangers, I never did finish my classes at seminary. A term short, I was. Perhaps that's why you felt my sermon this morning was, er, somewhat lacking. My poor mother was grief-stricken and quite ill, you see, and rather than spend the last of the money she gave me for my own education, I decided to pay for a doctor."

"And what happened to your mother?" asked Becky, leaning closer to hear the story.

"My mother . . ." At that point the reverend broke down in sobs. His shoulders shook, and his head bobbed with the effort of continuing his story.

"The physician could do nothing to save my mother. She passed to eternity two years ago, her heart still broken from the tragedy of losing my father."

"I'm so sorry." Becky whispered this time.

"No, it is I who am sorry," sniffled the reverend. "And I'm so ashamed of leading you astray. But you see, it had been my mother's dream to see me wearing my collar. 'Charles,' she told me, 'I die happy just knowing you've been ordained to the ministry.' You understand how I couldn't bear to tell her that the last of our funds had been spent on the doctor's fees. Not in her fragile condition."

"We understand." Becky nodded.

I don't, thought Patrick.

The Reverend Christie smiled weakly, as if he were recovering from the flu. "I knew you would, in the very same way you understand the needs of poor souls all around you." He twirled around with his arms raised, accidentally hitting the Old Man in the nose.

"Oh! Pardon me, sir."

The Old Man rubbed his nose and frowned but didn't answer as the reverend went on.

"Well, as I was saying, ever since my poor mother's death, you see, I've been preaching the gospel to the needy people of Australia." He raised his voice as he had during his odd sermon. "Such a need, don't you agree?"

Becky was still nodding. Patrick frowned.

"I understand your concern." The man looked directly at Patrick. His eyes were sharp now, without a trace of tears. "But for the sake of the lost, and for the remainder of our voyage together, perhaps you will still find it in your heart to call me 'Reverend Christie.' It was, after all, my mother's dying wish. To honor her, not me . . ."

"Reverend Christie," echoed Becky. It was her yes.

"And if I promise you," he continued, "as I promise God, that I *will* find my way back to seminary to honorably complete my schooling, perhaps you will hold this secret between us?"

His voice begged for them to agree, but Patrick wasn't ready to give in to a man who had lied to them so easily before.

"That would be fine." Becky's eyes were misty as she held her course.

"I knew I could count on you." The reverend smiled and backed out of the wheelhouse. His eyes twinkled as they had before. And then he was gone.

"What a heartbreaking story." Becky took Patrick's elbow once again. "I feel sorry for him, don't you?"

"No."

"Reverend Christie," snorted their grandpa. "I remember running into a 'Reverend Anton' once. I think it must have been in Goolwa. He sold snake oil and fake medicines. Relieved two of my crew out of a month's wages."

"Don't you believe Reverend Christie?" Becky looked at them with wide eyes.

"Didn't say that directly." The Old Man checked to see if the reverend was gone. "Keep your eye on the river. Shallow spots coming up."

For once, Patrick and his grandpa seemed to be on the same side of an argument. Reverend Christie was no pastor, after all, at least not a real one. And something told him the smooth-talking, teary-eyed man was very different from what Becky thought he was.

"He seems to enjoy the open air, in any case." The Old Man pointed down at their passenger, who stood on the forward deck, the wind in his hair. With a hand to shade his forehead, he scanned the distant shoreline.

"What is he looking for?" Patrick wondered quietly. He tried to pick out any sign of life in the trees, but for miles there was nothing except the occasional bright green or yellow flash of a parrot or the high-pitched screech of a pink galah parrot. Once in a while, down on the river, he noticed a bark aborigine canoe, and although most of the aborigines along that part of the river didn't look up when they passed, a few did wave. Finally Patrick began to see a few more small cabins on higher ground, away from the flooded fields and high water.

"Wentworth coming up," said Becky, checking the rolled chart. The Old Man looked down at their passenger and chuckled.

"Your *Reverend* Christie is going to fall into the Murray if he leans out any more."

"Does he see someone?" wondered Patrick.

As if he heard the question, Reverend Christie leaned back away from the water at the front of the boat and squinted up at the wheelhouse.

"I assume we're not stopping at the next town?" he yelled up.

"No reason to," replied the Old Man. Reverend Christie smiled and went back inside. Patrick heard another shout, Reverend Christie saying something to Mr. McWaid in the engine room. For a moment he thought it sounded like, "The captain said increase to full speed," but he decided that couldn't be right.

But it wasn't long before their speed began to increase and the steady wash of the paddles turned faster and faster. The Old Man cocked his head to the side and frowned.

"What's going on down there, Johnny?" he hollered over the railing. "Slow down!"

But their father didn't respond. The reverend was nowhere to be seen, either. And up ahead . . .

"Grandpa!" Becky called from her post at the steering wheel. "There's someone up the river who wants us to stop. And it looks like he has a gun!"

"What?" thundered the Old Man. He leaned forward and squinted. "What's going on?"

"Two men in a small launch," said Patrick. He could hardly believe what he was seeing. "One of them looks like a constable. And he's pointing a rifle at us!"

"Johnny!" The Old Man leaned out the side of the wheelhouse and yanked on the cord in the corner to blow the *Lady Elisabeth*'s whistle. If Becky didn't turn, they would collide. But the men up ahead only shouted and waved more wildly, the one with the gun waving it so they could see.

"I've seen those men before," said Becky, and Patrick recognized them, too. Could they be the same two men they had seen back at Swan Hill?

"Slow it down to quarter speed, Johnny," ordered the captain, but the paddle wheels continued to spin at full speed. "Do you hear?"

Still there was no response from down below, not even from Patrick's mother, who had been helping her husband.

"Patrick," said the Old Man, "run down and see what's wrong with your father. We have to slow down!"

"Yes, sir." Patrick was about to obey, but the Reverend Christie was hurriedly climbing up the ladder.

"Christie!" shouted the Old Man. "What's going on down there?"

The reverend shook his head and threw up his hands. "We're

113

doing all we can, Captain. Something must have stuck in the machinery."

Patrick tried to follow his grandpa's orders and slip downstairs, but the reverend stopped him.

"Don't go down there, boy," warned the man.

"But we have to stop!" Becky nearly screamed as she pointed directly ahead. Less than a minute, Patrick guessed, and they would crash right into the other boat.

"We are not going to stop, young lady." Reverend Christie's voice was level and steely, and he stood tall in the doorway. "I made sure of that. Now, run them down."

"You're daft, Christie," objected the Old Man. "Completely crazy! One of 'em's got a shotgun pointed our way and looks like he aims to use it."

Patrick tried to slip past Reverend Christie to see what was happening with his father, but the man pushed him roughly backward. Patrick toppled into his grandpa.

"Now, see here!" objected the Old Man, helping Patrick back to his feet.

"I'd hoped it wouldn't come to this," said Reverend Christie, a black glint in his eye. "You all seemed like such pleasant folks." As he spoke he reached into his coat and produced a shiny revolver, the kind used by outlaws and bushrangers. No one moved when he pulled back the gun's hammer with a horrible click.

"Sorry to disappoint you, sister." The man said to a wide-eyed Becky as he grabbed Patrick by the shirt with his free hand and leveled the gun at him. "Steer straight for that miserable little boat just ahead. In fact, I want you to ram it."

"I will not!" cried Becky, but the ugly gun at Patrick's side said otherwise.

"No time to chat about that now," answered Reverend Christie. Patrick didn't care for the view he had of the gun. He could hardly breathe.

"But . . ." Becky worried through clenched teeth. "Everything you told us was a lie?"

The father killed by bushrangers, the dying mother . . . The thought flashed through Patrick's mind, as well. *All lies*.

"Doesn't matter now." Reverend Christie, or rather, *Mr*. Christie, kept a straight face except for his dark eyes, which darted from them to the boat ahead.

"What are you, Christie?" demanded the Old Man. "A thief? Or worse?"

"Let's just say I'm a traveling man, living by my wits. Large bank withdrawals are my specialty."

"A bank robber," whistled Patrick.

"And pretending to be a pastor was your way of escaping the law," added Becky, her lips pressed together with rage.

"It's *you* they're after!" continued the Old Man. "That's what this is all about, isn't it?"

Even if he had wanted to, Christie didn't have time to answer. A shot like a cannon blast exploded from the river, directly ahead of them.

CHAPTER 15

DECEIVED

"Down!" cried the Old Man, and for a very short moment Patrick forgot about the gun Mr. Christie had pointed at him. As wood splintered just above their heads from the shot, Patrick lost his balance, turned his ankle, and shouldered the attacker out the side door of the wheelhouse. With a cry and a splash, Christie tumbled off the left side of the boat.

Did I do that? wondered Patrick, watching the man disappear. Becky crouched down but still held on to the steering wheel. Everything had happened so quickly.

"Where is he?" asked Becky. Patrick did his best to see outside through the open side door. It looked to him as if the *Lady Elisabeth* and her barge had sideswiped the boat with the two men. In any case, the other boat was right behind them now, still afloat, heading for the shore. The barge had swung out to the side of the paddle steamer and plowed into the mud.

But the Right Reverend Mr. Charles Christie had disappeared.

"I don't see him," said Patrick, still scanning the riverbank for a sign of the outlaw.

"There!" said their grandpa, grabbing the steering wheel from Becky and pointing at the water just behind and to the side. Sure enough, the impostor was swimming for all he was worth, straight toward the shore.

"The barge!" The Old Man nearly shoved Patrick out the side door, too. "It's aground. Untie the barge!"

Patrick could only obey. He flew out the door and down the ladder. For a moment he paused at the doorway to the engine room, unlooping the rope Mr. Christie had used to tie the doorknob shut. "Hello!" cried his father from inside, pounding on the door. Patrick undid the last loop and ran for the barge.

"Patrick, wait!" cried Mr. McWaid, pushing open the door, but Patrick was already running.

"I'll be right back, Pa!" he shouted over his shoulder.

"Hello!" called Jefferson, who stared at them from his perch on the wool bales. "We're aground, did you notice? And where's the passenger going?"

Patrick guessed he hadn't seen the whole drama with the men and the shotgun.

"We noticed," Patrick said to himself. But he had no time to yell back. He did as the Old Man had ordered and untied the barge, leaning dangerously over the edge to pull the last knot free.

"Hey, what are you doing up there?" yelled Jefferson.

"Sorry, can't explain right now." Patrick waved back and tossed the heavy line from the barge back into the river.

A moment later they were veering toward shore without the barge, with the Old Man at the wheel and still at full speed. Patrick hurried back to the wheelhouse.

"You're not getting away with this!" The Old Man shook his fist at Christie. Patrick's mother climbed up from the other side, and Mr. McWaid stationed himself at the front of the boat.

"What are we doing?" asked Patrick, but it was obvious as they circled around in front of the escaping swimmer. Behind them and to the left, the two men in their small launch had ducked around the grounded barge and were making their own chase. Maybe they thought they would head him off on the shore. The *Lady Elisabeth* and the other boat worked almost like a net to capture the escaping Christie.

"We're not going to reach him in time," said Becky, and Patrick could tell she was right. It wouldn't even be close; Christie was almost to the safety of the far shore.

"Faster!" The Old Man slammed his hands down on the wheel as if that would make the paddle steamer reach the escaping criminal sooner.

"Becky?" Their mother appeared at the door to the wheelhouse, concern in her voice. "Patrick? Will someone tell me what is happening? The reverend told us to go to full steam, and then we couldn't get out of the engine room. . . ."

"The Reverend—I mean, Mr. Christie—is not who he says he is," Becky explained matter-of-factly. "Those two men are after him for some reason. We're not sure why."

Patrick wasn't sure if his mother understood—or if he did. But they were nearly to the shore, and Christie had long since climbed out of the water and disappeared into the bush.

"Grandpa." Becky put her hand on the Old Man's shoulder. "He's gone, Grandpa."

At first the Old Man seemed not to hear, and he shook his head slowly, then squeezed his eyes shut.

"Are you all right?" asked Mrs. McWaid, but the Old Man would not or could not answer. His eyes still shut, he kept shaking his head slowly until they plowed into an overhanging tree and shuddered to a stop. That's when his knees folded underneath him like an accordion, and he crumpled to the deck.

"John!" cried Mrs. McWaid. "It's your father!"

She dropped to her knees where the Old Man had fallen onto the hard wooden deck, but Mr. McWaid hadn't heard her weak cries over the sound of the water and the still-puffing steam engine. The paddle wheels kept turning as the boat sat still, wedged against the riverbank. Patrick stood frozen in panic.

"Patrick!" cried his mother. "Go fetch your father. Quickly!"

But Patrick didn't need to move. A moment later, as the engine wheezed to a stop, their father was there, kneeling next to his wife and the Old Man.

"What happened?" asked Mr. McWaid. He put his ear to his father's chest and looked from face to frightened face. Becky touched her grandpa's forehead. At least he was still breathing.

"Grandpa was trying to run down that Christie fellow," explained Becky, "but then he shut his eyes and fell."

"Trying to run down Reverend Christie," repeated their father. "Tell me about that later."

"He's done it before," volunteered Patrick. "Actually, he keeps doing it."

"What?" Their father tried to make sense of it all.

"He's been having headaches and trouble seeing."

"You knew that?" Their father loosened the Old Man's collar. "I could see he wasn't feeling well, but I had no idea. Why didn't you tell us before now?"

The captain's eyelids fluttered weakly.

"I promised . . ." Patrick started to explain, and he looked to his sister for help.

"Don't blame the young ones, Johnny," whispered the Old Man. "It was me, made 'em promise to keep still. And it was quite a job keeping such a secret on this small boat."

He tried to sit up straight, but Mr. McWaid held him down.

"You stay where you are." Patrick's father sounded like a doctor. "And no more secrets."

"Just a dizzy spell, is all," insisted the Old Man, struggling to sit up. His eyes were only half open, and he looked confused. "An old person like me is entitled to a few aches and pains, is he not?"

"This is not just an ache or a pain," countered Mr. McWaid. "Something's wrong with you, and we're getting you to a doctor in the next town. That's the end of it."

This time the Old Man didn't argue, just mumbled to himself as Patrick and his father slowly helped him to his feet. But when he realized where they were, the Old Man's eyes snapped all the way open.

"What happened to that rogue Christie?" he roared, throwing off the arms that held him. "I almost had him. Why, if he thinks he can come in here and wave a pistol around like some kind of river pirate, then he'd better think again. . . ."

"He's gone, Grandpa," explained Becky. Only her soft voice seemed to settle the Old Man. "So are the two men in the boat."

She pointed to the launch up against the shore. "Why don't you just sit down, and we'll get you to a doctor?"

The Old Man sighed and puffed out his cheeks as he surveyed the scene around him. The two men with the shotgun had beached their boat and run after Christie. Jefferson and Luke waited patiently on the barge, still stuck on the midstream sandbar where they had gone aground.

Patrick couldn't help shivering when he looked up at the ceiling of the wheelhouse, where a stray pellet from the shotgun blast had ripped through the woodwork.

The doctor in Wentworth crossed his arms, then took a flat wooden spoon and poked at the Old Man's tongue. "Open wide!" he said, and the Old Man frowned but obeyed.

"Iss jhus uh dizzy shpell," explained the Old Man, trying to talk while the bespectacled doctor peered into his throat. The elderly doctor nodded. Patrick thought he was older than even his grandpa.

"Just a dizzy spell, you say?" he inquired, then poked and prodded some more with his spoon. "I'd have had a dizzy spell myself if that bushranger Christie had been holding a gun at me. And to think he was on your paddle steamer! Too bad he slipped away again. Why, I've heard he has a dozen disguises."

"Ahem." Mr. McWaid cleared his throat. "My father?"

"Ah yes, of course." The doctor turned back to the Old Man. He checked ears and eyes before he listened to the Old Man's chest through a hollow wooden tube, then counted his heartbeat while studying his pocket watch. The Old Man started to explain, but the doctor held up his finger to quiet the patient, then checked his temperature by feeling his forehead.

"The children say he's been having headaches," explained Mr. McWaid.

"Hmm." He looked in the Old Man's ears again and nodded seriously.

"Well?" demanded the Old Man.

The doctor turned to a shelf behind him and pulled down a large bottle filled with a clear liquid. He held it up to the light, adjusted his tiny spectacles, and grunted.

"You're running too hard," the gravelly voiced doctor finally told them. He looked seriously at the Old Man. "Pushing too much for a man of your age."

The Old Man rolled his eyes. "I've been working all my life. I can't—"

"Ah-ah." The doctor interrupted with a bony finger poked at the Old Man's chest. "You should rest and take this tonic for your dizzy spells. And you need to let your crew do some of the work instead of taking it all for yourself. Those days are over."

"Does that mean he's going to be all right?" asked Patrick, but the doctor didn't seem to hear, so he read the label on the bottle the doctor had given them:

Dr. Hostetter's Celebrated Bitters. A pure and powerful tonic, wonderfully powerful for correction of all manners of disease . . . prevents fever, fortifies the system against miasmas and the evil effects of unwholesome water, steadies the nerves, and tends to prolong life. Cures the sick or nervous headache, seasickness, cramps and spasms, and all other complaints.

That about covers it, thought Patrick, turning the blue bottle over in his hand before the doctor snatched it back and held it out to the Old Man.

"Try a spoonful of this twice a day," ordered the doctor. "But more than that, I want you to rest."

The Old Man shook his head as he buttoned up his shirt.

"We have only eighteen days to make Goolwa," he replied, stepping out of the tiny storefront room. "So enough of this foolishness. Let's go, Johnny."

Mr. McWaid took the bottle and shrugged. "I'm sorry, doctor. I'll see that he takes the tonic."

The Old Man slowly opened his mouth for the medicine, but he made a horrible face as Mrs. McWaid filled the spoon. He would not come down for his twice-daily dose of Dr. Hostetter's Celebrated Bitters, so Dr. Hostetter's Celebrated Bitters had come to him. Mrs. McWaid saw to it. With Becky standing by and Patrick at the wheel, though, the wheelhouse was getting crowded.

"My," said Mrs. McWaid, balancing the spoonful of syrup. "Fussing like this. You're worse than the children."

"Mother!" complained Becky.

"I meant when you were small." Mrs. McWaid smiled as she poured the bitters down her father-in-law's throat. He sputtered and complained, the same way he had at the doctor's office in Wentworth more than two weeks before.

I don't blame him, thought Patrick, catching a whiff of the medicine. It smelled like a mixture of castor oil and dead fish, and it turned his stomach inside out even from a distance. And as far as Patrick could tell, it wasn't helping his grandfather any.

"You're trying to kill me with that stuff is what you'll be doing!" complained the Old Man.

But Mrs. McWaid only smiled as she retreated from the wheelhouse. "Sit down now and rest."

"Rest, she says." The Old Man leaned against the wall of the wheelhouse and kept an eye on Patrick making his way down the river. "I'll rest if we make it to Goolwa in time."

Patrick already knew what would happen if they didn't make it to Goolwa by midnight. All those miles down the Murray, and it had come to this. They had pushed the *Lady Elisabeth* as fast as she could possibly go—Patrick knew that by the worried expression on his father's grimy face every time he had stepped out of the engine room. But still they had pushed on down the river, stopping in little riverside camps hardly long enough to catch their breath.

"Keep going!" the Old Man had told them, and they knew they must. Up with the dawn, and they were already steaming down the river, nearly full steam, sometimes until long after dinner. As the days became weeks, Becky had kept a journal of all the places they passed and a tally of the days left until they were due in Goolwa.

Each day they loaded firewood from the wood stops along the river, finished another lesson in geography or ciphering, and checked another day off Becky's list, until they were down to day thirty. The last day. Still no one had seen the *Gem* or any other sign of Warburton—not that Patrick had expected to.

Are we going to make it? Patrick knew well enough to keep the question to himself as they raced full speed across the waters, still except for a faint rippling of waves. Behind them they left a widening wake, and the twin waves from the *Lady E* and the barge seemed to go on forever now that the Murray had widened into what the chart called Lake Alexandrina. This was the widest and easiest part of their river journey before their destination, the river port of Goolwa.

But Patrick couldn't relax, and his grandpa paced nervously behind him.

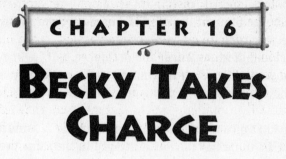

CHAPTER 16

BECKY TAKES CHARGE

"Can't we squeeze any more steam out of that boiler, Johnny?" the Old Man called down from his perch in the wheelhouse. "At this rate we're surely not going to make it by midnight."

Mr. McWaid was standing on the lower deck, taking a quick break from the engine.

"I told you we have serious problems with this boiler. I don't know how much longer I can keep it running."

"I hear what you're saying," replied the Old Man, "but we can't slow down. Not yet."

"But, Father, listen to me. It's a miracle she's not blown her seams already with the shape she's in. And if it blows . . ."

"Where did you learn all this about steam engines?"

"From you."

The Old Man frowned at his son's answer, but he wasn't going to be talked out of his plans.

"All right, then, ease off a couple of pounds. But don't let it below that. We have to keep going."

Mr. McWaid frowned, but he nodded and disappeared into the engine room.

"Maybe she was just underwater too long," muttered the Old Man, still pacing, obviously fretting about what might have been. Patrick bit his lip and stared straight ahead, trying to discover the shortest route to the far side of the lake, to Goolwa, the last town on the river before it turned into the sea.

Goolwa, he thought, turning the name around in his mind. *I wonder where such an odd name came from.*

Patrick didn't know much about Goolwa, but he knew all too well what would happen if they didn't make it there by midnight. If only they had another day. But the calendar couldn't be turned back.

"If I hadn't picked up that charlatan Christie . . ." muttered the Old Man. His mind had obviously strayed to the same thoughts as Patrick's. "That'll teach me for being the Good Samaritan."

"You didn't know. It wasn't your fault." The words that came out of Patrick's mouth surprised him. But the Old Man wasn't convinced.

"Well, the mistake cost us a whole day, it did. A day we could have used. Now, if we don't make it to Goolwa in time, we've lost the other half of the *Lady E*."

"I know that. But taking on Christie wasn't your fault."

"But it *was*," argued the Old Man. "I got what I deserved, taking on that fraud. We should have left him on the wharf in Swan Hill."

"But how could we have known?" asked Patrick. "He looked like a decent sort."

"Ministers, like I said," the Old Man spat out the words. "Not to be trusted, any of 'em. I knew it when I saw him."

Patrick swallowed hard, but he knew he couldn't let the comment pass.

"How can you say that?" Patrick felt his palms sweating and cold at the same time. "I know plenty of people with real faith."

His grandpa studied him out of the corner of his eye. "*Real* faith, is it? And what, pray, might that be?"

Patrick's throat went dry and his mind went blank at the challenge. "Well . . ." He struggled to explain what he knew was true. But all he could think of was the way down the Murray. The man who had stolen his grandpa's money. The accidents. The men who had taken advantage of Michael and taken the koala. And the "Reverend" Christie, who had made fools of them all. They hadn't come across many people who displayed real faith, it was true. Not that there weren't plenty of decent folks along the river. People who waved and smiled, who shared the latest news and a fish or two, and who wished them well.

"I suppose it's something like what you did for Michael," Patrick finally blurted out. He hadn't quite thought it through, but maybe it would make sense when he said it. The Old Man crossed his arms and watched him carefully.

"You remember when those two fellows talked him into selling his koala, and . . ."

Patrick didn't need to repeat the story; the Old Man was nodding. Yes, he remembered.

"Well, when you bought the koala back with the last money we had, I thought it was sort of, well . . ." Patrick searched hard for the right words—words that wouldn't sound like a pastor preaching a sermon. "Seems as if we're always running into trouble on our way down the river, but God is always finding us a way out. Just like you bought Christopher back when he was in trouble."

The Old Man returned to staring at the widening river ahead of them.

"If the Almighty is in the business of finding us a way out," he mumbled, "now's the right time for it."

Patrick couldn't argue with his grandpa on that point. Now *would* be a good time. He stared with his grandpa across the water. As the sun began its descent in the west, he lost his thoughts in the huffing sound of the steam engine and the constant splash of the paddle wheels.

Faster, he heard himself urging the old steam engine, the same way his grandpa had done so many times over the past few days. *Faster, or someone else is going to buy back this boat.*

But the engine of the *Lady Elisabeth* sounded weaker than ever, as if it were wheezing its final breaths, getting more and more tired the closer they got to their destination. And every time the thought crept into Patrick's mind that they weren't going to make it on time, he shooed it away.

Be gone! he told the thought. *We're going to make it on time. We must!*

As he stared ahead, a door slammed downstairs, and he heard a whistling come through the wheelhouse. The Old Man looked around in surprise.

"Hold on, boy," he told Patrick. "Looks like a bit of a breeze is picking up from behind us."

"A bit of a breeze" turned out to be one of the Old Man's quaint expressions, one that had only a tiny flavor of truth to it.

"Hurricane" would be more to the point, thought Patrick as the wind propelled them across Lake Alexandrina, hour after hour, picking up more speed the closer they got to their final destination. Toward the end of the afternoon, Patrick felt like a skipping rock thrown again and again across the lake.

"I like how we sail down the waves, Patrick!" said Michael, who had come up to the wheelhouse for a better view of the wild ride. "Whoosh! It reminds me of when we were on the ship in the ocean, coming to Australia."

Becky groaned quietly but didn't say anything. Michael didn't notice; he just pretended his hand was a boat as he showed them how the wind and waves had pushed them along all afternoon and into the early evening. Patrick didn't want anyone to remind him, either. He squinted through the early evening gloom and pulled his stiff hands off the wheels for the first time in hours. He ached all over from the wrestling match he'd had with the bucking paddle steamer. Only Michael had thought it some kind of game.

All I need is somewhere to stand that doesn't rock, Patrick told himself.

"We're just lucky the barge didn't take a bite out of us," said the Old Man, and Patrick knew he was right. With the waves and wind behind them, the barge should have slammed into them from behind many times. One time on a particularly nasty wave, Luke had to steer the big cargo almost even with the *Lady Elisabeth* just so they wouldn't crash.

But still they flew onward toward Goolwa, making up some of the time they had lost back on the river.

"Comfortable it's not," admitted the Old Man. "But I have to admit, we've made up a bit of time this afternoon."

"Here it is, six o'clock, and Goolwa's almost in sight," said Mrs. McWaid, who had come up for a rare visit to the wheelhouse. "We've six hours to spare, do we not, Captain?"

The Old Man had to nod his head yes.

"I assume the new owner is waiting for us," he told them.

Mrs. McWaid smiled. "You mean *half* owner."

As they spoke, the tired old steam engine downstairs wheezed, coughed hoarsely, then finally stopped. A moment later the only sounds they could hear were the sloshing of waves beneath them and the Old Man's shouting as he launched down the ladder to see what was the problem.

"Looks like our problems aren't over yet," said Mrs. McWaid.

She was right, of course.

"One of the pumps is acting up," announced their father. "Just what I was afraid of."

"Here we are, five miles from Goolwa," sighed Patrick, "and it might as well be a thousand. We're not going to make it."

Becky looked at her brother as if he had just sold them into slavery. "Don't say that. We'll make it. If we have to get out and push, we're going to make it."

But Patrick had almost talked himself into defeat. "Sure. The new owner is probably standing there on the wharf with a stop-watch and a smile, thinking about how the *Lady Elisabeth* is going to be all his in a few hours."

Patrick shook his head and gave himself permission to complain even more. "I don't know what kind of a silly deal it was that Grandpa had to get us here by midnight."

Below, they could hear the Old Man's grumbling through the floorboards. Three or four times someone tried to start up the engine, but it would only wheeze and die, cough and sputter. Becky looked around at the paddle steamer as they rocked in the wind. The barge had drifted up on its towline, and it had started to bang against the railing of the *Lady E.*

"We're going to make it!" The light in Becky's face told Patrick he'd better not stand in her way as she rushed past him, hopped over a couple of wool bales on the deck, and ran into the salon.

"We'll need this tablecloth," she said, yanking the waxed linen cloth off the table. A glass went flying, shattering against the wall. Patrick ducked.

"Rebecca Elisabeth McWaid!" exclaimed their mother, but Becky was already moving to the front of the boat, where the Old Man stored ropes, tools, tarps, and such. Mostly things for covering cargo on deck.

"I'm sorry, Mother." Becky offered the apology over her shoulder but didn't slow down. "I'll clean it up, but . . ."

"Honestly . . ." Their mother sighed as she picked up a few pieces of broken glass. Patrick followed his sister's parade of tarps.

"Becky, do you really think—" Patrick was starting to warm up to the idea—if it was the same one his sister had in mind. In the engine room the Old Man was still grunting and wheezing almost as much as the stalled steam engine.

"Of course," she replied, handing Patrick another tarp. "Here, hold this one. We'll spread them out in the main salon and sew them all together."

It just might work, thought Patrick as he dragged the heavy, smelly canvas back to the floor and pushed the table out of the way. He sneezed once, then again. The material smelled of mildew; most likely it hadn't completely dried out since the boat had been underwater.

"Here, now," said Becky, following him into the salon. She threw her load down on the floorboards next to Patrick. "All we need to do is sew these together."

A few moments later they had turned the salon of the *Lady Elisabeth* into a busy sailmaker's loft. Becky directed the stitching together of four large pieces of canvas into one. Patrick and his mother worked feverishly from opposite ends, trying to see who would be the first to reach the middle of the huge sail. Michael tried his best to keep Christopher the koala from walking all over everything.

"Make the stitches tight enough so it won't come apart," warned Becky. With a sharp knife she sliced off a side that would have made the sail lopsided and uneven.

But we don't have time, thought Patrick. *This is going to take hours.*

Meanwhile, Michael scurried back and forth to the supply locker, bringing back every pole he could find. Most were only five or six feet long, and Becky sent him right back to search again.

"Longer," she told him. "It has to be at least twenty feet long, like the sail."

"Aye, aye!" Michael saluted his sister and ran back to search for another pole.

Behind them, the wind was still nudging their barge, bumping it into the back of the paddle steamer. Once in a while Patrick caught a glimpse of Luke fending the barge away with his legs.

"There it goes again." Their mother noticed another bump. Patrick kept stitching, trying to make his fingers fly.

"Not bad, little brother." Becky smiled as she watched his handiwork. "For a boy."

"You can't afford to be choosy right now," replied Patrick. She smiled and straightened out the corner of their sail.

"Well, look at this," declared Jefferson as he stepped into the salon. "It looks like—"

"It's a sail, Jeff," interrupted Michael. He carried in another pole from the storage locker. Still too short. "All we need is a long pole to string it up with."

"You don't need a long one." Jefferson picked up two poles. "Just lash a few of these together. Here, I'll show you."

With that Jefferson joined the desperate sail-making crew, though he had to run back every few minutes to help Luke with the barge. When they were finished more than an hour later, they had a huge patchwork-quilt sail to go with three poles that Jefferson had expertly tied together.

"These two we tie together for a mast," he explained. "Like an Indian tepee, only with just two poles."

Becky nodded. "Then the third pole we hang sideways at the top."

Patrick could picture it in his mind by that time. "That will be the one that holds the sail."

All that was left was to test the idea.

"It's a good idea," said their mother, straightening up from her knees and setting her big needle carefully on the salon table, "but it may just rip to shreds."

With the wind still whistling outside and only a few hours left, Patrick was afraid that's just what would happen.

CHAPTER 17

UNDER FULL SAIL

"You really think it will hold?" Michael was the only one who dared ask the question, though Patrick was sure they were all imagining what would happen when they unfurled their sail into the evening. The two-piece mast was in place on the top of the wheelhouse, tied with two ropes from behind and two in front. The sail itself was tied together with a piece of cord, wrapped tightly in place but ready to be pulled from the deck below. And when that happened . . .

"Can't see that there's much chance of it working," remarked the Old Man. Mrs. McWaid looked at him with the fierce expression of a mother bear protecting her cubs.

"Of course," stammered the Old Man, working hard to cover his tracks, "I'm supposing there may be just as much chance for it working as not."

"That would make it the first time the *Lady Elisabeth* was a sailing ship, I'll bet." Jefferson stood with his hands on the ropes that held their mast in place.

"Well, then, what are we waiting for?" It was Michael again. "Can I pull the cord?"

"It was Becky's idea," suggested Jefferson.

"No, it was Ma and Patrick who did most of the work," countered Becky.

"Will somebody just pull the cord and take the blame?" muttered the Old Man. "And let's see if the thing works."

Patrick held his breath as Becky held the cord. At the last moment, though, she handed it over to him.

"Here. Hurry."

Of course, Patrick wanted to see the sail unroll as much as anyone there. He tugged at the cord and watched in wonder as checkerboard, blue gingham, then white sheets rolled down from their position on the crossbeam.

Instantly the wind caught a corner of the unrolling sail, and the center billowed out. Everyone cheered.

"It works!" cried Michael. "The sail really works!"

"Did you expect it not to?" asked Luke, grinning and clapping from his spot on the barge. As the sail filled and tugged against the two ropes they had tied to its bottom two corners, the barge seemed to drift farther away. They actually were picking up speed. Maybe walking speed, maybe a bit slower, but at least they were moving.

"Well, how about that." The Old Man shook his head and almost grinned.

"It works, Pa!" shouted Michael to Mr. McWaid, who was still in the engine room, working on the leak in the cranky steam engine. "It really works . . . so far."

Even Patrick couldn't help smiling as he shook his sister's hand in congratulations. They were moving. Really moving. The wind saw to that.

The smile drained from Becky's face, though, when she looked up at the wheelhouse.

"But no one is steering!" she yelped, and Patrick raced her up to the steering wheel. He grabbed it in time to keep them from going in circles.

From here on to Goolwa, he told himself, *this is the sailing vessel* Lady Elisabeth.

"The only remaining question is . . ." began Becky, but she didn't have to finish. Patrick knew by the dark color of the sky that they wouldn't have much time to sail to their destination. He guessed it was somewhere around seven-thirty. And he could imagine the paddle steamer's new owner pacing the wharf and grinning.

"Faster." This time it was Becky who whispered the command as they pointed the nose of their paddle steamer once more directly toward Goolwa. They would just follow the wind and surf their way home. Simple, but not easy.

In fact, the steering wheel was harder than ever to control, and the paddle steamer rocked awkwardly under its new sailing rig. They were moving, it was true, but only half as fast as they had been under steam. And the hurry-up seams they had stitched in the heavy fabric could rip apart at the next big puff of wind.

Their grandpa was down in the engine room grumbling and shouting at the engine, threatening it with horrible things if it wouldn't cooperate and start up just once more. And it was steadily getting darker.

"Is that it?" Becky wondered a couple of hours later. She pointed off to the side at some lights.

For a moment Patrick panicked. "Can't be! Goolwa's supposed to be straight ahead!"

This time they didn't have their grandpa to ask, so Patrick kept steering his way forward, the way he had been told to. Besides, he was pretty sure their course was straight ahead—unless the wind had shifted.

"I think the wind has changed," suggested Becky. "We need to turn."

Patrick still wasn't sure, but by that time there was nothing ahead of them but darkness. Off to the right and ahead, he could make out the twinkling of lights Becky had pointed out.

"Patrick?"

"All right." He changed course. "But what time is it?"

"Doesn't matter. We're going as fast as we can. If we don't make it, we don't make it."

"We could get out and swim."

Becky didn't answer. At least the lights were growing brighter. As usual, she had been right.

"Goolwa dead ahead!" shouted Michael from the bow. Patrick

hadn't noticed his little brother standing out there in the dark. "Almost there, Patrick."

Maybe we'll make it after all. Patrick allowed himself the small luxury of imagining themselves tied up to the wharf in Goolwa in time to save their paddle steamer. Up ahead, the twinkling lights had turned to lanterns, and he could make out the shape of just one paddle steamer. Goolwa, it seemed, was quiet that night.

"I give up!" shouted the Old Man, and his voice rumbled throughout the quiet paddle steamer. "He can have this old wreck, for all I care. She's been underwater for weeks, and the old engine won't hold steam any better than I will. And there's a hole in the bottom, to boot!"

They could hear him grumbling to himself as he climbed the ladder up to the wheelhouse, but he fell strangely silent when he stood behind Patrick and Becky.

"And what town might that be?" he asked, his voice hollow and emptied of the fire they had just heard.

"Well, Grandpa, you can check it on your charts," began Becky. "But we're pretty sure it's—"

"Man alive! I know where we are, girl. I just don't quite know how we got all this way flying your tablecloth to the wind."

"I knew it would work, Grandpa," insisted Becky.

Patrick felt almost as surprised as his grandpa but kept his mouth shut and steered for the wharf as the Old Man told him. He was afraid to ask the time.

"What about letting Jefferson steer us in?" asked Becky, looking over her shoulder to see if Jefferson was down on deck. "He knows a bit about bringing a ship into the wind."

"Humph." The Old Man turned back into his ornery self. "I imagine we can handle this just fine without any outside help."

"Can you see, then, Grandpa?" asked Becky.

The Old Man shook his head slowly. "Don't need to. I'm rememberin' it plain as day. Now, you'll notice the wharf up ahead. . . ."

Patrick steered toward the dim lights of the town, relying on his recollection of the place—the same place where they had begun their journey up the river months ago. The Old Man helped by giving details about shallow spots to look for and the best place to tie up on the wharf. All with his eyes closed.

"Get ready to swing the barge over, boy!" the Old Man hollered out the side door at Luke. Their quiet aborigine friend had been faithfully holding the barge in tow and on course ever since the wind had taken hold of their homemade sail.

"We're ready back here!" Luke hollered back. Jefferson stood on the deck of the *Lady Elisabeth*, ready to throw a mooring line to the two men who waited on the wharf.

Patrick gritted his teeth, wondering how they were going to stop. No brakes, no paddles to put them in reverse. Just the wind, blowing harder than ever. It seemed as if they would ram the Goolwa wharf. Unless . . .

Patrick was the last to hear the ripping sound and realize what was happening. A moment later the checkered tablecloth from the makeshift sail was flapping crazily, covering the front of the wheelhouse and blocking what little view he had. The masts came thumping down on top of them.

"Oh no." Patrick didn't know which way to steer. Of all the times for the sail to collapse . . .

I might as well close my eyes, like the Old Man, Patrick thought for a moment, but Becky had already jumped outside. She sprang like a cat to the roof, ripping away their sail.

"I need some help!" she cried, and Patrick could hear the sail flapping wildly. *What would it take*, Patrick wondered, *for the wind to pick her up off the boat and send her into the river?*

The Old Man must have wondered the same thing, because a moment later he had disappeared outside to help wrestle down the sail.

"Can you see now?" he roared from up on the roof. Patrick could, and what he saw made him want to jump overboard with the sail that Becky and their grandpa had just tossed into the water.

"Left, LEFT!" cried the Old Man.

Patrick had the sinking feeling that he had been in this situation once before. Something hard was rushing at the *Lady E*, and there was not much he could do to keep them from crashing. Last time it had been the huge log on the flooded Murray River, the one that had sent the poor paddle steamer to the bottom. This time it was the dark shape of the Goolwa wharf. Patrick guessed that another crash would probably have the same result.

Not again! he whispered as he turned the big wooden steering wheel all the way to the left. Even with the sail gone, they were bearing down on the wharf as if they couldn't—or wouldn't—stop. He spread his feet to brace himself, waiting for the sound of splintering wood.

It never came. Only a whoop from behind them as the barge swung around sideways and back up into the wind. Like the tail of a kite, the barge moved. Luke had managed to wag his way out just enough to pull them back from a sure crash.

"Grab the line, please!" shouted Jefferson as he tossed his ropes to the waiting men.

Even in the darkness Patrick thought he saw the white gleam from one of the deck hand's teeth. He had to be grinning.

"Sweetest landing I've ever seen," said the fellow. "Sail or steam. That's a right tricky approach, coming downwind like that."

"Right-oh," agreed the man next to him. They pulled in their lines, and the wind gently wedged both the paddle steamer and the barge into place. "That's a fair piece of seamanship, mate."

"It wasn't me," replied Patrick quietly, but he couldn't point to anyone else in the wheelhouse. His grandpa patted him on the back and gently pried his fingers off the steering wheel.

"Well done, boy. We made it, thanks to you and your sister's crazy sail."

"But what time is it?"

Becky jumped down to the deck in a whirlwind of skirts, and the Old Man slowly pulled out his pocket watch.

"Well, now, I can't say for certain. Seems to have stopped a few miles back."

"You mean we've been pushing to get here by midnight, and we don't even know for certain what time it is?"

Their grandpa sighed and leaned against the doorway for support. No one but the two men on the wharf had come to meet them. No new owner with his stopwatch and a grin on his face. The Old Man sat down on the deck, exhausted. Had they made it in time?

CHAPTER 18

A FORTUNE GAMBLED

It was up to Patrick, Becky, Jefferson, and Luke to find out whether they had met the deadline.

"You don't know what time it is, do you?" Patrick asked the two men who had helped them tie up to the Goolwa wharf.

One shrugged and looked at his partner. "Eleven, twelve . . . I don't carry a pocket watch around."

"Patrick!" Their father leaned over the railing and pointed to him. "And you, too, Becky. Stay on the wharf for now. We'll find out what's happening in the morning."

"In the morning?" Patrick couldn't believe it. "But how will the new owner know we made it here in time?"

"He'll know sure enough." Mr. McWaid returned to helping his father get down the ladder from the wheelhouse. "We've got people who saw us arrive. These two gentlemen, for instance."

But the two gentlemen were gone, and the wharf was silent except for the sound of the wind-lapped waves that washed against the shore. The town was silent, too, with only a few dim windows in the distance. One was the railroad station; Patrick remembered it was across the tracks that led to Goolwa from the coast, from the ocean port of Victor Harbor. The other light must have come from a hotel of some kind, and he thought he saw a face staring at them for a moment from his window before pulling back into the shadows. It was a wonder they had found Goolwa in the dark, he thought.

"If he's not here now," said the Old Man, "we'll find him in the morning. We've done our part."

"Have we?" Patrick turned to the others. Maybe his grandpa was right. But there were still too many loose ends for Patrick to relax: Who was the mysterious new half owner of the *Lady E*, the one who was supposed to meet them but hadn't? And besides that, what had happened to Warburton, the thief who had stolen all of the Old Man's money?

Jefferson pointed with his nose toward the other paddle steamer. A lone lantern hung on the afterdeck, where a man in a chair rested with his feet up and his face tucked into a wide-brimmed hat. On the side of the wheelhouse, the lantern light flickered just enough for them to read the name. The *Gem*.

"I don't know about you," whispered Jefferson, "but I think we need to pay a visit to that boat."

"We can't." Becky checked the lines one more time to make sure the boat wouldn't drift away.

"Why not?" wondered Patrick. "This may be our chance."

The four of them sat on the deck of the *Lady E* while Mr. McWaid disappeared ashore to check in with the harbormaster.

"He said not to leave the wharf," reasoned Jefferson. "And you wouldn't be doing that. Besides, you don't want me and Luke to go over there all alone to capture the thief, do you?"

Patrick thought for a moment. Now that they had finally caught up with the man they had been chasing all the way down the Murray River, he was pretty sure he didn't want to meet up with him after all. On the other hand . . .

"Becky, Patrick," their mother called softly out the window of the *Lady Elisabeth*. "Get inside now. It's late."

"We'll be right there, Mother," replied Becky. She looked from her brother to their two friends. "If Mr. Warburton is here now, he'll still be here in the morning."

"Not if he sees the *Lady E*," whispered Jefferson. "He'll turn right around and run. But come to think of it, I'd sure like to see the fella's face when he catches an eyeful of this paddle steamer!" He laughed softly and pretended to jump back with fear. "He's going to think he's seeing a ghost!"

The others laughed along with him, but there was no escaping Mrs. McWaid's watchful eye.

"You two boys come along now, too," she told them. "It's been a long day for everyone."

Patrick followed his sister back to the paddle steamer, knowing there was no way he would be able to sleep—even though his body was aching and sore all over. For what seemed like hours, he thrashed and turned, throwing the covers off and listening to the night. In the distance he heard laughing. Was it Warburton coming back to the *Gem* for the night?

Not likely, Patrick told himself. *Warburton is probably long gone. Surely he's not sleeping on another paddle steamer only a few feet away*. Patrick decided that would be too much of a coincidence.

Patrick kept up that argument with himself for what seemed like hours. He prayed, he talked to himself, he tried to sing a song silently to himself. But that only made him think about the time they had sung a few hymns with Mr. Christie.

Now I really won't be able to sleep, he thought, *thinking about that fake*.

Still, "Be Thou My Vision" kept ringing in his head, especially the line "Riches I heed not, nor man's empty praise. Thou mine inheritance, now and always . . ."

Maybe that's just the right song for us, Patrick thought a little sadly, *since Warburton probably took our riches anyway*.

Still singing in his mind, he finally dozed off.

The sound of a cheery steam whistle blew in Patrick's ear, startling him awake. "Wh-what?" Patrick sprang up, feeling like a jack-in-the-box. His eyes were wide open, but he wasn't even sure who he was, much less where he was or what was happening.

But there it was again, and the second cautious blast of the steam whistle.

Steam whistle! thought Patrick as his mind began to unfog. The deep tone of the whistle told him it wasn't the *Lady Elisabeth*. Besides—he remembered now—the *Lady E*'s steam engine wasn't working.

"Did you hear that?" Patrick asked as he sprang out of his bedroll, but there was no one to answer. Becky was already gone, and Michael only rolled over in his spot and buried his head under a blanket. Outside, though, it was the beginning of another beautiful, cloudless day. By the time the sun came up, Patrick guessed it would be even warmer than the day before.

"What took you so long?" whispered Jefferson, who stood with Becky on the edge of the wharf in the dark pink light of early dawn. Seeing the hair sticking up straight on Jeffereson's head, Patrick supposed he had just rolled out of bed, too.

"What do you mean?" asked Patrick, and he lowered his voice when he saw a man on the other paddle steamer fussing with a couple of mooring lines.

Black smoke rose from the *Gem*'s twin smokestacks. She was a bit longer than the *Lady E*, with more windows and more room on deck. She was definitely cleaner. The captain, the same man they had seen sleeping on a deck chair the night before, stood impatiently on the upper deck. He was a well-dressed man in his fifties, looking very proper in a pressed blue suit and captain's hat. Unusual for the river.

Who's he waiting for this time of the morning?

"Jeff and I have been taking turns," explained Luke. He whispered, too. "Nobody's left the *Gem* all night."

"Or come back from town, for that matter." Jefferson put his hands on his hips and stared right at the captain.

"Well?" Patrick scratched his head and led the way. "Now's our chance, then, isn't it?"

The captain eyed them as they approached, but he didn't seem to care much that four young people were boarding his paddle steamer.

"Act as if we know what we're doing," whispered Patrick over his shoulder. He slipped on the wet deck, but Becky caught him from behind.

"Can I help you?" asked the captain, stepping down from the upper deck. He looked impatiently at them, then at his pocket watch.

"Yes, sir." Patrick was the first to answer. "We're here to meet with a Mr. Warburton."

Becky, Luke, and Jeff peeked around from both sides of Patrick.

"You, too?" replied the captain. He gave his watch another glance. "I told him we would be sailing at six. Said he was just going up for a meal!"

"So he's traveling on this boat?" asked Jefferson.

"That he is. Now he's gambling away a fortune, I imagine."

Patrick groaned. They had found the slippery Mr. Warburton, or they almost had. But they were probably too late to reclaim any of the stolen money.

"Can we wait for him here?" asked Becky. She ran her hand along the polished mahogany railing.

"Suit yourself," the captain answered as he climbed the stairs leading to his wheelhouse. "Though I don't know what a mob of children would have to do with such a character. And you'll need to be off this vessel when we leave the wharf."

The whistle blew again, this time just above them. Not more than a minute later, they saw a man in a white suit running their direction.

"Reminds me of Christie all over again," whispered Patrick.

"Where have you been, Warburton?" thundered the captain of the *Gem*. "We were ready to put out without you."

"But I was winning!" cried the man as he jogged across the wharf.

Once he got closer they could see that the rather short, well-dressed man wore dark black circles under his droopy eyes, as if he hadn't slept. His clothes were wrinkled, and his black patent leather shoes could have used a good shine.

"Are you Mr. Warburton?" asked Patrick, moving forward to

meet the man as he stepped aboard. He still wasn't sure how to begin. Should he say, "Hello, you stole my grandpa's money," or "How much money did you steal from my grandpa?"

Either way, Patrick guessed it wasn't going to be a pleasant conversation.

And Mr. Warburton didn't look like a pleasant man. His breath smelled of stale cigar smoke and beer, and his collar was way out of place. He looked curiously at the greeting party.

"Jonas Warburton," he answered in a clipped English accent. "What can I do for you?"

"I'm Patrick McWaid." Patrick tried to look straight into the man's eyes, but he couldn't. "We've been following you—"

No! Patrick scolded himself quietly. *That was the wrong thing to say.*

"I mean, we've been wanting to ask you a couple of questions but haven't been able to catch up with you since Echuca."

That was a little better. Except that I made it sound as if we're police inspectors.

"Me?" asked the man. "What do you *children* want with me?" His eyes widened as he caught sight of the *Lady Elisabeth*.

"You used to be a crewman on the *Lady Elisabeth*, isn't that right?" This time it was Becky's turn to be the inspector.

Warburton craned his neck forward as if he were seeing the *Lady E* for the first time.

"The *Lady* . . ." Warburton's mouth dropped open. "I thought surely the Old Man had died."

"What's that?" asked Patrick.

A crewman hopped to the wharf and began untying one of the lines that held the *Gem* in place.

"He's our grandpa, and he's not dead," answered Becky. "We were just wondering if you had any idea what could have happened to a sum of money he—"

"Let's go!" shouted the *Gem*'s captain while the deck hand struggled to untie another rope.

"Sorry, skipper," shouted the deck hand. "But someone's gone and tied a hundred sailor's knots in this line."

Jefferson covered a grin with his hand but stood away from the ropes. Warburton tried to push away from them.

"Listen, I'd like to help you, and I'm glad to see that the Old Man's boat is afloat again, though I surely hadn't expected it. But as you see, this boat is leaving."

"What about the money you stole from him?" Patrick squared himself up against the man and caught his breath. He hadn't planned on coming right out and saying it quite like *that*, but there it was.

"Uh, he didn't quite mean it that way." Becky tried to stand between the two, but Warburton ignored her.

"Did I hear you correctly?" The man's nostrils flared. "You think *I* stole the Old Man's loot?"

"Well?" It was too late for Patrick to back down. Warburton met his gaze, nose to nose, then his mouth began to quiver, and he burst out laughing. Patrick certainly wasn't expecting *that* reaction.

"You followed me all the way down the river for *this*?" Warburton's face turned red as he nearly doubled over in shrieks. "What did he say about me? Did he say I stole the money? Because if he did, he's even crazier than I thought."

"He didn't say that *exactly*," Patrick admitted. Suddenly he felt very small and silly for blurting out what he had. *What if Warburton is telling the truth?*

"Well, then, what *did* he say?" Warburton demanded.

"He doesn't quite know what happened to the money," said Becky.

"That's just what he told *us*." The man stabbed at the air. "Here we were, trying to help him raise that boat of his . . ." He pointed at the *Lady Elisabeth*. "And he promised us pay and a half."

"What happened?" asked Becky.

The man threw up his hands and snorted. "Nothing! Never saw a shilling, and the Old Man was acting like a lost puppy. Some of us thought there never *was* any money."

"But there was," insisted Patrick. "We thought it was stolen from him."

"There was no stealing." Warburton pulled out his empty pockets to prove his point. "I give you my word on that. Unless you count the card games lately, wherein I've nearly lost the shirt off my back."

Maybe it was the sad, tired look in the man's eyes, but Patrick found himself starting to believe what Warburton was telling them.

"But what about all that money you've been spending?" asked Jefferson. "All the way down the river, they say . . ."

The man laughed again. "I try to win more than I lose." He winked at them and pulled a playing card from the sleeve of his coat, an ace.

A gambler, thought Patrick. *And a cheat, at that. But a thief?* He wasn't so sure anymore.

"Look, I felt as bad as anyone for leaving him," Warburton went on. "But men were getting hurt. There was talk of a curse, even, though I never believed that. I was just between games, and I needed the work."

"So why did you leave him?" wondered Becky.

Warburton seemed to notice the hurt expression on her face, and he put out his hand. "Look, miss. Some of us have to make a living, and that doesn't include mothering an old river coot who's losing his marbles. No offense intended, but—"

This time the *Gem*'s whistle cut through the morning air, long and loud.

"Got it, Captain," cried the deck hand, finally holding up the rope. "Someone really knotted that one good." He turned to Patrick and the others with a stiff expression.

"You four," he said with a pointed finger. "Pay your fares or get off!"

Patrick turned to Becky, then to Jefferson and Luke, who had already started toward the wharf. "We'd better go . . ." suggested Becky. "What else can we do?"

Patrick didn't know exactly what he had wanted the man to say or do, but this was definitely not it. He turned with the others to leave.

"I'm sorry about your grandpa," said Warburton, "but there's nothing else I can do."

"Thank you for your help, Mr. Warburton." At least Becky was polite.

"Good to see the *Lady Eliza* floating," said the gambler. Patrick didn't bother correcting him. They jumped off the *Gem* just in time.

"Now what?" he wondered aloud, not expecting an answer. Out of the corner of his eye, he glimpsed a barrel-chested man hurrying their way. He looked more weathered than the men they usually saw working on the river, and his wild hair clearly hadn't seen a comb in recent days.

"Gates!" Luke shouted and sprinted toward the man before Patrick knew what was happening.

CHAPTER 19
MYSTERY BUYER

"Boomer Gates!" The Old Man slapped the other man's back as they stood in the salon of the *Lady Elisabeth*. "Why, I never thought I'd see you again!"

His voice trailed off, and Patrick was surprised to see his grandpa's eyes mist.

He's not crying, is he? wondered Patrick. Boomer Gates smiled back at the warm welcome.

"How did you find us here?" asked Luke. "Did you just—"

Gates shook his head and smiled.

"No coincidence, son." He looked at Luke, who was obviously not his son. Patrick had heard the stories, though, of how this man, a lighthouse keeper, had raised Luke after the young boy's parents had died. That had been out on Kangaroo Island, the place Patrick and Jefferson had washed ashore when they had first come to Australia.

"Then how did you catch up with us?" The Old Man put everyone's question into words.

"Just wanted to come check out my new investment," answered Gates, a twinkle in his eye. He paused for a moment to see what effect his words would have.

"You?" The Old Man's eyes nearly popped out of his face. "No! Can't be!"

"Gates!" Luke's head nearly hit the ceiling when he jumped. "I didn't know you had so much money."

"Lot of things you don't know about me, son."

"So you're the mystery buyer." Patrick didn't believe it. Couldn't believe it. Not the Gates they knew. Not the crusty old man who had taken them in and brought Patrick to the mainland to find his parents.

"Boomer Gates." This time the Old Man looked far away, as if he were remembering an old story. "Who would have believed two old convicts would finally become partners." Then his expression clouded over, a sudden storm.

"You really bought the other half of the *Lady E*?"

"That's what I've been trying to tell you, you old fool." Gates gave the Old Man a good-natured shove with his elbow, but the Old Man seemed to lose his balance. Mr. McWaid supported him from behind.

"When?" asked Luke.

"After you left with Jefferson for Echuca," the man explained, "I decided to spend a couple of days in Melbourne. Take care of some money matters."

"I never knew you had any money." Luke still looked as surprised as everyone else. Gates smiled.

"Other people spend. I save. But, uh, all those years, I never paid much attention to where my money was invested. At least, not until a couple of months ago. Not until I heard about a strange old man who owned a Murray River paddle steamer. Fellow by the name of McWaid."

The Old Man smiled like a little boy as Gates continued his story.

"I said to myself, 'I used to know a McWaid,' and the banker, he told me this McWaid fellow was needing an investor, on account of his paddle steamer was on the bottom of the Murray River and needing a bit of repair."

Gates ran his finger along the ceiling and looked at the way the paint had peeled.

"I can see he was right about the repair part."

The Old Man paced the floor. "What I still don't understand is why you made it such a big secret. Why didn't you tell us what you were doing? What was the reason for this deadline?"

"Let me finish my story, you old convict." Patrick figured the man could get away with calling his grandpa a convict since he himself had once been one, too.

"As I was saying," the man continued, "this banker told me about this investment, and I took most of my money and poured it into this boat. But I still couldn't believe it was you, and I didn't want anything to hold you up. Not after all these years. That's why I insisted you get here by yesterday."

The Old Man chuckled. "And then you weren't even here to see us arrive, right on time."

"I was here." Gates pointed toward the hotel where Patrick had seen the dim light, the person who had been watching them in the night.

"But the secrecy?" The Old Man didn't quite understand. Neither did Patrick.

"I wasn't one hundred percent sure it was you," replied Gates. "Although I knew there weren't too many Patrick McWaids in the world, I didn't want to make a complete fool of myself before I was completely sure."

"Ah, too late for that now." The Old Man was ready for a joke, and they laughed together.

"You once told me about your wife, Elisabeth, which made me think that the *Lady Elisabeth* was surely yours. Aside from that, though, I wasn't sure you wanted to see old Boomer Gates again. You did a pretty good job of disappearing as soon as we were both set free. When was that, now, back in—?"

"Don't remind me."

"Oh no, you're not getting off that easy, McWaid. You saved my life once."

The Old Man tried to wave off the remark, but he could not.

"Yes, you did save my life, and I've been in debt to you ever since. Now's my turn."

The two friends went on like that, back and forth, reliving old memories of how they had come to Australia, swapping stories about what had happened to them since. Gates smiled when he told of his life on Kangaroo Island, how he had found Luke, and how he and his wife—before she had died—had taken him in.

When it was the Old Man's turn to tell of his life on the river, though, the stories came more slowly, the words sometimes scrambled. At times it looked as if it hurt to speak.

"And then . . ." The Old Man paused for a breath and closed his eyes for a long moment while everyone waited.

Patrick wrinkled his brow and looked at his father. *He's getting worse*, Patrick wanted to say out loud, but he would save it for later.

"Ah, well, you know, perhaps it wasn't such an important detail." The Old Man tried to smile, but Patrick could tell he had to be in pain. "I'll remember it again later. It appears we have plenty of time to swap stories again, does it not?"

"That we do!" Gates clapped his hands. "But I see there's more work to be done here than you told me."

"Well . . ." the Old Man began. "Without the funds, it's been a hard go."

"Oh, that reminds me, Grandpa," Becky interrupted. "We caught up with Mr. Warburton. He was on the *Gem*."

"Warburton?" The Old Man looked at his granddaughter as if he was hearing the name for the first time.

"That's right," added Jefferson. "And he's either a very good liar, or he really didn't steal the money we thought he did."

"I'm not so sure . . ." said Mr. McWaid.

"No, Johnny." The Old Man shook his head slowly. "I never really believed he stole the money. He seemed decent enough. I'm just an old fool."

"Please don't say that, Grandpa," pleaded Becky.

"I'm only telling the truth of the matter now, lass, because I've thought about it and thought about it all the way down the river."

"But—" interrupted Mr. McWaid, but the Old Man held up his hand and continued. "I lost the money, and that's all there is to it. 'Tis the only thing that could have happened."

"So you honestly don't think it was stolen?" Jefferson couldn't seem to believe his ears. The Old Man just kept shaking his head.

"No, lad. Perhaps I lost it in all the confusion when we were refloating the boat, before you all came to help. But no one stole it, far as I can tell. So there's no one to blame but me, and that's the end of it. I just didn't want any of you to worry about me."

Mr. McWaid frowned but didn't argue anymore. Gates looked as if he didn't know what to say.

"Well, we're not losing anything else," said Patrick, trying to change the subject. "And we're getting the *Lady Elisabeth* repaired properly now, right?"

"Of course, we'll need a new boiler, to be sure," said Mr. McWaid. "And several parts need replacing, along with new gauges and—"

"Enough." Gates crossed his arms and smiled. "I can see that we'll need a complete and proper refitting before heading back up the river."

"Here in Goolwa?" wondered Luke.

Gates shook his head no. "I'm thinking we stop by the island on our way to Adelaide, then get the work done in the city."

Patrick could hear another paddle steamer coming to roost at Goolwa. But no one on the *Lady Elisabeth* said a word.

"Did I say something wrong?" asked Gates, looking around at his audience.

"You're saying we should go outside?" asked the Old Man. He looked concerned as he twisted a hard crust of bread between his hands.

"We're always outside, Grandpa," said Michael. "What's wrong with going outside?" He had been listening quietly. It was about time for one of his questions.

"Yeh, outside." Gates laughed and turned to the youngest McWaid. "By outside, your grandpa's meaning out in the ocean, like. That's what rivermen call anything outside the mouth of the Murray."

The Old Man shook his head. "I've only done it once before. The bottom's always shifting, Boomer Gates. You know as well as I do that it's a dangerous idea."

Boomer Gates would not be argued with. "If you're half the seaman I've heard tell you are, Captain Patrick McWaid, then I'm sure you could manage with your eyes closed. And with this fine crew . . . I say we make what repairs we can here and not waste any more time. On to Adelaide!"

Luke and Jefferson cheered for the new voyage. Patrick wasn't sure he was supposed to, but he clapped his hands, too.

"On to Kangaroo Island!" boomed Gates.

The next week was filled with as much excitement as Patrick could remember, now that Boomer Gates was aboard as half owner. Becky and her mother hurried about as they had before, making sure that fresh supplies were loaded aboard. Patrick and Jefferson unloaded the wool from the barge and from the deck of the *Lady E*, and Michael ran errands for everyone. Only Luke seemed a little distant, and even though he helped as much as Jefferson, he did a lot of staring and daydreaming, watching the seabirds and watching for something in the distance.

The Old Man was another story.

"I'm taking my medicine, aren't I?" he asked when anyone appeared overly interested in his health.

"I think we ought to take you back to the doctor," announced Mr. McWaid the day before they were scheduled to leave. He pushed his chair back from the salon table. "Your dizzy spells are coming three or four times a day now, aren't they?"

"Not more than once in a great while," retorted the Old Man, finishing up another piece of bread.

"Well, your vision, then," cut in Mr. McWaid. He put up two fingers. "How many fingers do you see?"

"Oh, so now you're a doctor, are you, Johnny? I'll not be treated like a child."

"Ah, but if you act like . . ." Mr. McWaid stopped in mid-sentence, then sighed as he thought twice about what he was going to say.

"Grandpa," Becky bravely joined in the argument, "all Father is trying to say is that you're not getting better. Whatever's ailing you is getting worse."

The Old Man's expression softened when he looked across the table at his granddaughter, but he obviously wasn't giving up.

"Becky, my dear, I've been to the doctor. And he just relieved me of tuppence for the good pleasure of telling me I was an old man." He thumped his fist on the table, and Becky jumped back. "I don't need any doctor to tell me that!"

"You're a stubborn old fool, Patrick McWaid." Gates stood up. "I'd be the last one to get involved in a family matter, but—"

"Then don't." The Old Man took a swig of his medicine, corked it back up, and slammed it on the table. "See? There's an extra dose of the good medicine the fine doctor prescribed for this old man. Isn't that what they've always called me? The Old Man? Well, now the title fits!"

Gates left the room without another word. The Old Man wiped his mouth with the back of his hand and looked around.

"What's everybody staring at?" he asked. "If we're leaving tomorrow, there's still a sight of work to do."

Becky dabbed her eye with a napkin but didn't move. Finally Patrick threw down his napkin and followed his father to the engine room. His grandpa was right about one thing. There *was* plenty of work to do.

CHAPTER 20

OUTSIDE

"How will we know the way?" Patrick asked as they gathered speed and pointed the *Lady E* toward the final leg of their journey down the Murray. At last they were on their way "outside."

"Just keep us pointed toward those dunes." Gates lifted his rough, cracked hands and pointed straight ahead. It didn't look right to Patrick, but he wasn't going to argue. Gates grinned.

"I know it doesn't look like much, son. There's times when a man can wade across the mouth of this river."

"But you think we're going to make it out all right?"

Gates nodded, sure of himself. "You just follow where I tell you to steer. We'll make it fine."

Patrick checked with his grandpa, who was sitting on a crate in the corner, his mouth turned up and a peaceful expression on his face.

"Hey, Patrick!" Michael flew in. "Are we really going out into the ocean—"

"Shh!" Patrick warned his younger brother with a finger to his lips, then pointed to their grandpa.

"Oh, sorry." Michael tiptoed in, which made Patrick chuckle, considering all the other noise from the water and the steam engine. The Old Man didn't move.

"He seems pretty tired," began Gates, looking back with a touch of concern. Patrick knew what he meant.

"He's been like that more and more, ever since . . ." Patrick's voice trailed off as he wondered how much to say. But he needn't have worried—Gates had turned his attention to something else.

"I'm still not so sure about that engine." Gates turned his head, listening to the chugging and whirring through the floorboards. "Even after the repairs we made. I'm hoping it holds out until we can get it replaced in Adelaide."

Patrick nodded. A minute later Gates headed for the door himself.

"I'm going down to check on that engine. Think you can hold it on this course? Tell me if you need anything."

"I'm fine, sir."

Gates studied Patrick's face for a moment. "Of course you are."

The man disappeared down the ladder, and Patrick returned his attention to the course ahead. The wind was picking up a little, with a puff here and there that seemed to rock them. At least they weren't towing the tipsy wool barge anymore. But it still didn't look to him as if there was any way out. All he could see was a low range of hills—sand dunes, maybe—sheltered by a dull gray mist.

"Are we going to crash, Patrick?"

Patrick jumped at Michael's question. He had almost forgotten his brother was standing next to him.

"We're not going to crash."

"Grandpa wouldn't let us, would he?"

"Grandpa's asleep."

Something in Patrick's voice must have sounded sharper than he had meant it to sound.

"Why are you always mad at Grandpa, Patrick?"

"I'm not mad. It's just . . ."

He paused, but Michael just looked at him expectantly.

"I guess I wonder sometimes . . . if he'd been more careful with his money, maybe all this wouldn't have happened."

"You make it sound terrible. This trip is fun, isn't it?"

"Uhh . . ." Patrick thought for a moment about all the things his brother didn't know, about the missing money, about their grandpa being ill. Things he didn't think Michael would understand. Patrick hadn't looked behind him for a few minutes, so his grandpa's voice startled him even more than Michael's had.

"You've still not pardoned the Old Man, have you, lad?"

Patrick jumped, which brought a chuckle.

"Didn't mean to startle you."

"I wasn't startled."

"And you're a terrible liar."

Patrick swallowed hard at what his grandpa said, but he didn't turn around.

"You've not forgiven me for losing the money?" the Old Man repeated his question.

"No, sir. I mean, yes, sir. It's all right."

"No, you've not done it, or I would have known."

Patrick wasn't sure how to answer or how to say that he didn't really understand a word of what his grandpa was telling him.

"I know something about pardons," continued the Old Man. "See, I received a pardon of sorts once. A piece of paper that said I had served my sentence after five long years. I'd been sentenced *seven* years for stealing a sheep back in Ireland."

Patrick looked over his shoulder, but only for a brief second. He could not interrupt the tears that now flowed freely down his grandpa's cheeks.

"But I'll tell you something: That pardon meant no more chains, no more prison cells, no more guards watching over me. And I knew that when I walked away with that pardon in my hand, I wouldn't be coming back. Not ever. Do you see what I'm trying to tell you, lad?"

Patrick started to nod, but it changed to a "no." He still didn't follow, and the Old Man closed his eyes.

"Ah, Boomer Gates is right. Maybe I *am* an old fool."

"You're not . . ."

"Isn't that what you think?" The Old Man allowed himself a smile for the first time. "Isn't that what you both think? The Old Man's a cranky old fool. Lost all his money. Mad at the world. Doesn't even go to church, for goodness' sake."

Why is he saying all this? Patrick and Michael stared at their grandpa with openmouthed wonder.

"Well, I've never told anyone." The Old Man winced in pain as he sat on his crate, his eyes tightly shut. "Not a soul, mind you. Would ruin my reputation as a tough paddle-steamer skipper. But Elisabeth knew. She, your grandmother, she was a fine woman."

"I know . . ."

"The thing is, I went to mass when I was a lad." It sounded like a confession, the way the Old Man said it. "And after we were married, Elisabeth, she always insisted on going every week. Before your father was born."

The Old Man smiled at the memory. "She used to read the Bible to me, and . . . we prayed together, she and I."

Patrick wouldn't have interrupted for anything.

"That surprise you?" The Old Man finally opened his eyes again, and they glistened with tears.

"No," Patrick stammered. "I mean, yes. . . ."

"Well, I know in my heart that I believed back then." The Old Man's soft voice cracked. "And I suppose I still do. It was just so . . . so hard after she died. Like a light went out for me."

"I'm sorry."

The Old Man smiled. "Well, now, so am I. I know I've never acted like a good Christian—certainly not like you and your sister. I suppose it's always just been easier to play the part of the tough old captain."

"That's all right, Grandpa."

"No, it's not all right. But were it mine to do over, I would have done a lot of things differently, I suppose. Now it's too late for all that. What did I expect?"

He was asking himself. This time the Old Man leaned his head way back, as if he were searching for the stars.

"I've thought about it lately," he went on. "And I don't expect you or anyone else to ever pardon me for the hurt I've brought this family."

"Grandpa—"

"No, let me finish, lad. Confession is good for the soul, and you're the closest thing to a priest I have just now."

Patrick sighed and nodded as the Old Man continued.

"I know it was a long time ago, long before you were born, but you've a right to hold it against me. The stealing that brought me here to Australia in chains. And then never answering all your father's letters, I . . . I . . ."

Patrick said nothing as his grandfather struggled for words.

"But like I said, I can't expect your pardon now, Patrick. You've every right to be angry."

Finally Patrick knew what he had to do—what he had to say. It was not in himself to say it, but say it he must.

"I'm not angry anymore, Grandpa. I do forgive you. I really do. And God forgives you. For everything."

For everything . . . Patrick remembered the times his grandpa had dragged his family into doing things they hadn't wanted to do. The times when the Old Man had seemed more like a dictator than his father's father. Patrick supposed there were plenty of things to forgive his grandpa for—there was no need to remember them all. They were past.

"Patrick?" came his grandpa's soft voice, so soft and weak it frightened Patrick.

He looked back at his grandpa, who was holding his forehead in pain.

"Grandpa!" cried Michael, stepping over to help. "You're going to be all right, Grandpa. You said so yourself. Just dizzy spells, is all."

"I was lying." The Old Man put his hand up, then let it fall. "I don't know that I'm going to get better."

"But—" Patrick couldn't believe what his grandpa was telling them.

"Shh, now, listen closely."

Patrick felt hot tears sting his eyes as his grandpa's words sunk in, but he did as his grandpa asked. He listened.

"Look for soft spots between the breakers."

Patrick wasn't sure what "soft spots" were, but his grandpa went on.

"And follow Jefferson's lead. He'll tell you how much water you have under your keel."

Patrick didn't like the way his grandpa said "you" and "your" instead of "we" and "us." *As if he won't be on the boat anymore . . .*

"Keep your speed up, and don't slow down for anything once you get into the breakers. Don't turn around, don't show your beam to the sea."

"Beam?"

Patrick's grandpa smiled once more. "You've been with this old sailor this long, and you still don't know what 'beam' means? Side, boy. Don't show your side to the waves, or you'll roll the *Lady E.* And I wouldn't forgive you for that."

"No, sir. I'm sure you wouldn't."

Down on the deck, Jefferson pulled up the lead line and pointed to the right a bit with his thumb. The lead line was a long line— sort of like a clothesline—with a lead weight at the end. Jefferson coiled it into his left hand and threw the lead weight out with his right to figure the depth of the water. Patrick eased the wheel over to follow the deeper water of the channel.

"That's it." The Old Man seemed to see where they were going, even with his eyes closed. "You're following the channel. Me, I think maybe I'm not meant to leave the Murray. Maybe that's a good thing."

"No, it's not, Grandpa." Patrick didn't like the way the conversation was going. It sounded too much like "good-bye." The Old Man pulled back when Gates breezed into the wheelhouse.

"We're down to two fathoms," he announced, keeping his eyes focused on the roiling water ahead and on the whitecaps and breakers that threatened to push them back.

"Two fathoms," repeated Patrick. He could feel his heart beating faster. *Which way to steer? What did Grandpa tell me?*

"That's twelve feet, boy," the Old Man whispered in Patrick's ear. "A fathom is six feet."

"Right." Patrick knew it couldn't get too much shallower before they bounced on the bottom and, depending on how strong the waves were, broke up into kindling. He didn't need to know how deep a fathom was to understand the power of the breakers ahead. Jefferson waved again.

"Fathom and a half," he called back. The stiffening wind caught his words and snapped them at Patrick, the same way it hurtled the seabirds coasting around their heads.

At least our steam is holding up, Patrick told himself. But as they began to plow through the freshening surf and felt the surge of the sea beneath them, the steam engine gave a cough and hushed, deathly still.

"Not again," groaned Patrick, remembering the approach to Goolwa. With the wind in their face, this time they would not be able to cheat their way through. "This engine knows exactly the wrong times to quit!"

Patrick wrestled with the steering wheel, but the rudder was useless. Without power they surely would turn their side to the waves, as the Old Man had warned him against doing, and flip over.

"Hold it there!" commanded Gates. The Old Man said nothing, and Patrick was more than afraid to turn around and see why not. He gripped the useless steering wheel while Gates sprang down to the deck to help Jefferson. Down in the engine room, Patrick could almost feel his father sweating over the ancient engine, begging it to start. A larger wave caught hold of the front end, nudging them sideways.

One or two more like that, thought Patrick, *and we're going to turn over*.

Down on the forward deck, Jefferson, Luke, and Gates struggled with an anchor, trying to get it untangled from a mess of chain. When a wave broke with vengeance and green spray over the front of the paddle steamer, Jefferson glanced up at Patrick with a look that said he could use another hand.

"Go ahead." Patrick jumped at his sister's voice. He hadn't heard her come up beside him. "I'll try to hold it here."

"Thanks." He was glad to let his sister take over. But he didn't have to leave the wheelhouse after all because the *Lady E*'s steam engine suddenly popped to life.

"Ha-ha!" laughed Patrick, waving his arms in the air. The others on the deck answered with a whoop of their own, and Becky grinned from ear to ear. The Old Man sat motionless behind her, leaning halfway against the back wall.

"Grandpa?" Patrick shouted above the engine. "Are you . . ."

The Old Man smiled. "Sounds good to me, too, boy. Now, show your sister what I just told you about steering into the waves."

It took both of them to hold the *Lady Elisabeth* steady through the vicious ocean waves, both their concentration to hold the right course through the shallow channel and the confused waves that now started to come at them from several different directions. And there was still a ways to go before they were safely out of the ocean waves.

Down below and up front, Jefferson balanced with the swells from his spot on the bow, flinging out the lead line and shouting back how deep the water was. Gates teetered next to him, holding on to his shoulder and helping him read the knots in the cord that told them the water's depth.

"That's close, lad," worried Gates. He cupped his hands around his mouth to make himself heard. "We've only inches to spare."

"We'll make it," said Becky, but Patrick wasn't so sure.

"Patrick."

A gray-backed gull wheeled overhead, laughing at them with a sharp *kwarr-kwarr* just before the *Lady Elisabeth* slammed against the bottom of the river.

CHAPTER 21

TO BE HOME

"That's it!" yelled Patrick, and for a moment he wondered if they would have to swim for shore.

"Hold your course, son!" called the Old Man. His hoarse voice was nearly drowned out. They bounced again, and the *Lady E* shuddered. Patrick gritted his teeth as he and Becky clung to the wheel.

"Keep going!" Patrick urged the boat as Becky helped keep the wheel steady. Whether there was water enough under them to keep them afloat, or whether the waves tossed them over like a pancake in a griddle, they couldn't do anything about it.

It's in your hands, God, Patrick sent up a silent, desperate prayer. *Just like everything else.*

"Patrick," the Old Man whispered weakly. "Patrick, are you there?"

Patrick glanced quickly to see his grandpa staring at him.

"I'm here."

"Are you on course?"

A swell picked them up in its gentle grip, and Patrick held his breath, waiting for the deadly thump. This time, though, they didn't meet the bottom of the shallow river delta.

"We're on course, Grandpa. We'll make it fine, just the way you said."

The Old Man didn't answer for a few minutes, only sat quietly and smiled to himself. Patrick thought he heard him humming.

"Did you—" Patrick began, looking back and forth between the course he had to keep and the past he had come from. His Irish grandpa was smiling wider than he had ever seen him smile.

"I heard you, Grandson," said Patrick's grandpa. "I heard you just fine."

Becky slipped away from the wheel then, her face pale.

"I'm going to get Pa," she said. "He should be here."

"Ah yes." Their grandpa nodded, his eyes seeming to stare off in the distance. "That would be a good thing. We can sing our way out the Murray."

It seemed to Patrick a very odd time to be singing, indeed.

"What's wrong with a little merriment?" asked the captain of the *Lady Elisabeth*. A few minutes later he had propped himself up on his crate and sat with his arm around his son as they paddled slowly out to sea. Patrick's parents had left the fussy engine on its own for a short while. Luke and Jefferson crowded in, too, along with Gates.

A sea breeze ruffled the Old Man's wild silver hair.

"Johnny, what about playing your tin whistle?" he whispered. "What about a tune?"

"No." Mr. McWaid kneeled next to his father. "You should rest. You're not—"

"Rest?" The Old Man chuckled, and they leaned close enough to hear. "Not when I have a chance to sing at me own wake. How many other men are blessed with such a thing? Tell me that."

"Don't talk so." Mrs. McWaid tried to quiet the Old Man, but he would not be quieted. So Michael brought up the tin whistle from below, and with tears in his eyes, their father began to play. Patrick had a hard time steering, but at least the way had opened up and he didn't have to worry so much about staying in the channel.

Their grandpa sang in a hoarse, low, husky voice with what had to be the last of his strength. He sang in his ancient language from Ireland, the Gaelic that Patrick had never learned.

" '*Gus fuair mé litr ó mo mhíle ghra . . .*' "

Soon Patrick recognized another tune, one his father had sung for them a long time ago in English.

" 'I'll spend my days in endless roving,' " Patrick added his voice to the melody and his grandpa's Gaelic whispers, " 'soft is the grass, my bed is free. Ah, to be home in Carrickfergus, on that long road down to the sea. . . .' "

They sang their grandpa's song again three days later, standing stiffly on the bluff overlooking the ocean and the narrow passage of emerald sea that lay between mainland Australia and Kangaroo Island. Kangaroo Island, where Luke had said he wanted to stay and help Gates with the lighthouse, where the grass smelled soft and green, like in their grandpa's song. It wasn't Carrickfergus, and it was surely a long way from Ireland, but it *was* pretty.

They would continue on to Adelaide in a couple of days, as it was not far down the coast. Gates had promised they would get a new boiler for the steam engine there and put the *Lady Elisabeth* into top shape. But not before they buried their grandpa there on the hill, on a spot Michael had chosen that overlooked a small harbor Luke called Wallaby Bay.

"He would have liked the view," said Becky, and her voice caught. She crouched down and placed a yellow spring flower on the fresh grave, a flower she had picked in a meadow as they walked up the hill from the seaside town of Kingscoate. Her tears watered the blooms she left there.

Patrick didn't think he had any tears left. No anger left, either, especially not at his grandpa, stubborn as he had been.

There's just no good in being mad, thought Patrick, and he thought back with a smile to his grandpa singing "Carrickfergus" in the last hours before he had died. It was a sad song, but his grandpa hadn't seemed sad. And he remembered his grandpa's words to him, as well: *"I know in my heart that I believed. . . . And I . . . still do."*

Patrick stood beside his sister, looking off toward the low, distant mainland and trying to figure if he could see the mouth of the

Murray from where they stood. It would have been nice, he thought, if they could.

But he couldn't see, maybe from the mist on the bright blue ocean, maybe from the mist in his eyes. All he could see was Luke's Wallaby Bay.

"I'll come by once in a while." Luke rested his hand on Patrick's shoulder. "Put some flowers on his grave. And maybe you'll come back to the island to visit, too?"

Patrick breathed in the sweet wind of Kangaroo Island and nodded. He would like to do that. He would miss Luke, and it would not be easy to say good-bye again.

"That would be very nice," said Mrs. McWaid, smiling at their friend. She gave them all a few more minutes to stand in the sun before turning away with Mr. McWaid.

"I'd like that," added Patrick.

Slowly they followed Mr. and Mrs. McWaid down the hill. No one was in any particular hurry, and Gates was the first to interrupt the steady sound of the wind that whistled up from the brilliant blue waters of Wallaby Bay.

"I'll be happy to help you over to Adelaide," he told Mr. McWaid. "But after that, what do you think? Do you want to find another crew? Sell your half of the *Lady Elisabeth*?"

No one answered.

"I'm sorry, perhaps it's not the right time to be asking such a question." Gates ran a hand through his hair. "It's just that . . ."

"No, that's fine. This is the proper time." Mr. McWaid gazed at the harbor, where the *Lady Elisabeth* looked strangely out of place among the few ocean-going boats: a small coasting schooner with two masts, an old fishing boat anchored just offshore, and a handful of rowboats pulled up on the beach.

"We're not going to sell the *Lady Elisabeth*, are we, Pa?" As usual, it was Michael who asked the question that was on everyone's mind. This time, though, it didn't take long for their father to answer.

"No, Michael." Mr. McWaid shook his head. "Somehow, it wouldn't seem right."

"What, then?" Gates looked confused. "Pardon me for asking, but what about a captain and crew?"

This time it was Becky who spoke up.

"We can run the boat, Pa. You know we can. Grandpa taught us."

By the way his parents looked at each other, Patrick was sure they had been thinking the same thing. He had noticed the same look dozens of times before when they were about to say, "Well, all right, but . . ."

"Patrick and I can take turns steering," Becky continued. "We know the shallows and the snags and . . ."

"I'll help you with the steam engine, Mr. McWaid," volunteered Jefferson. "The new one."

"And I'll help with . . ." Michael pressed his lips together and tried to think of something he could do. "I'll help with the ropes."

Mr. McWaid smiled and put his hand on Michael's head.

"Looks as if you have a crew, Captain," Gates told their father. "Again, I probably shouldn't say this, but if it helps your decision any, I've already arranged for the boat to carry a cargo of sugar, flour, and rice up from Adelaide to Echuca as soon as we're refitted. We'll be making a profit."

Mr. McWaid looked from his wife to his three children, then at Jefferson and Luke, and finally at Gates.

"I'm not going to make that kind of decision unless you're all agreed. It's one thing to ride a paddle steamer down the river, but it's another thing to live on the boat and make it your life."

"I think we should at least try." Their mother's voice was soft but sure. One by one, everyone else agreed. All except Patrick, who couldn't quite find his voice.

"As half owner," Gates put in, "I wouldn't trust the *Lady Elisabeth* to anyone else. And what's more, the Old Man would have told you the same thing. I'm sure of that."

Patrick followed the man's gaze back up to the hill. He could see the white cross they had planted there, next to a lonely tree that was just starting to lend its shade. A tiny songbird perched on the cross and offered a hymn that floated down the hillside. And Patrick knew that Gates was right.

"I'm for it, too," Patrick agreed. "Grandpa would have wanted it this way."

EPILOGUE

AUSTRALIA AS IT REALLY WAS

Wild gold rushes, tippy wool barges, escaping criminals . . . Was it really all like that? It's safe to say that yes, quite a few of the adventures Patrick, Becky, and Michael experienced in this story actually happened some time in the 1860s.

Maybe not all at once or to the same people, of course. But old diaries and books about the Murray tell us plenty of interesting tales. Wool barges did make their way up and down the river, and men steered them as Jefferson and Luke did. Accidents happened, too, much like the one where the top-heavy barge flipped. That was before they had a lot of safety regulations or rules that required captain's licenses. (Remember how the Old Man was afraid of what officials would do if they found out he didn't have one?)

The scene with "Doctor Hostetter's Celebrated Bitters" is based on a real newspaper advertisement, found in a copy of the old Riverine Herald (which, by the way, is still published in Echuca). That newspaper also says that people did search for gold on the Murray Flats, though they never quite found it there. The "Reverend" Christie incident really happened, too—and that was the actual (fake) name the escaping outlaw used for himself!

History is like that—full of color and characters. And life on the river during the last half of the 1800s was anything but boring.

Just ask the people who worked and lived on the Murray River paddle steamers.

Be sure to read Book 6 in the exciting
ADVENTURES DOWN UNDER!
Firestorm at Kookaburra Station

A stop in the river port of Wentworth proves to be much more than Patrick, Becky, and Michael expected after Michael stows away in a runaway balloon and they meet a strange silent man who helps find their way back to safety. The McWaids find they must work together as never before to make a living, but the real test comes when an out-of-control firestorm approaches. As they try to escape the flames, Patrick must face fears he never knew he had!

From the Author

One of the best parts about writing is hearing back from readers—so please feel free to ask me a question or just let me know what you thought of the adventure. You can drop me a line, care of Bethany House Publishers, 11300 Hampshire Avenue South, Minneapolis, Minnesota, 55438. I'll look forward to hearing from you!

Robert Elmer

Series for Middle Graders* From BHP

ADVENTURES DOWN UNDER · by Robert Elmer
When Patrick McWaid's father is unjustly sent to Australia as a prisoner in 1867, the rest of the family follows, uncovering action-packed mystery along the way.

ADVENTURES OF THE NORTHWOODS · by Lois Walfrid Johnson
Kate O'Connell and her stepbrother Anders encounter mystery and adventure in northwest Wisconsin near the turn of the century.

AN AMERICAN ADVENTURE SERIES · by Lee Roddy
Hildy Corrigan and her family must overcome danger and hardship during the Great Depression as they search for a "forever home."

BLOODHOUNDS, INC. · by Bill Myers
Hilarious, hair-raising suspense follows brother-and-sister detectives Sean and Melissa Hunter in these madcap mysteries with a message.

GIRLS ONLY! · by Beverly Lewis
Four talented young athletes become fast friends as together they pursue their Olympic dreams.

JOURNEYS TO FAYRAH · by Bill Myers
Join Denise, Nathan, and Josh on amazing journeys as they discover the wonders and lessons of the mystical Kingdom of Fayrah.

MANDIE BOOKS · by Lois Gladys Leppard
With over four million sold, the turn-of-the-century adventures of Mandie and her many friends will keep readers eager for more.

THE RIVERBOAT ADVENTURES · by Lois Walfrid Johnson
Libby Norstad and her friend Caleb face the challenges and risks of working with the Underground Railroad during the mid–1800s.

TRAILBLAZER BOOKS · by Dave and Neta Jackson
Follow the exciting lives of real-life Christian heroes through the eyes of child characters as they share their faith with others around the world.

THE TWELVE CANDLES CLUB · by Elaine L. Schulte
When four twelve-year-old girls set up a business of odd jobs and babysitting, they uncover wacky adventures and hilarious surprises.

THE YOUNG UNDERGROUND · by Robert Elmer
Peter and Elise Andersen's plots to protect their friends and themselves from Nazi soldiers in World War II Denmark guarantee fast-paced action and suspenseful reads.

*(ages 8–13)